IN THE WILDERNESS

Manuel Rivas was born in A Coruña in 1957. He writes in the Galician language of north-west Spain. He is well known in Spain for his journalism and television programmes, as well as for his prize-winning short stories and novels, which include the internationally acclaimed *The Carpenter's Pencil*.

Jonathan Dunne is the translator of Manuel Rivas's *The Carpenter's Pencil*. His other translations from the Galician include the poetry of Rosalía de Castro and the short stories of Rafael Dieste.

ALSO BY MANUEL RIVAS

The Carpenter's Pencil
Vermeer's Milkmaid & Other Stories
Butterfly's Tongue

Manuel Rivas

IN THE WILDERNESS

TRANSLATED FROM THE GALICIAN BY
Jonathan Dunne

VINTAGE

Published by Vintage 2004

2 4 6 8 10 9 7 5 3 1

Copyright © Manuel Rivas, 1994
Copyright © Grupo Santillana de Ediciónes, S. A.
English translation copyright © Jonathan Dunne, 2003

Manuel Rivas has asserted his right under the Copyright,
Designs and Patents Act, 1988 to be identified as the author
of this work

First published in Galician by
Ediciós Xerais de Galicia in 1994
and in Spanish by Editorial Alfaguara in 1998

First published in Great Britain in 2003 by
The Harvill Press

Vintage
Random House, 20 Vauxhall Bridge Road,
London SW1V 2SA

Random House Australia (Pty) Limited
20 Alfred Street, Milsons Point, Sydney
New South Wales 2061, Australia

Random House New Zealand Limited
18 Poland Road, Glenfield,
Auckland 10, New Zealand

Random House (Pty) Limited
Endulini, 5A Jubilee Road, Parktown 2193,
South Africa

The Random House Group Limited Reg. No. 954009
www.randomhouse.co.uk

A CIP catalogue record for this book
is available from the British Library

ISBN 0 09 945518 8

Papers used by Random House are natural, recyclable
products made from wood grown in sustainable forests.
The manufacturing processes conform to the environ-
mental regulations of the country of origin

Printed and bound in Denmark by
Nørhaven Paperback, Viborg

Fierce crows of Xallas
who wander far,
in the wilderness,
with no today or tomorrow,
would that I could keep you company
o'er the vast expanse!

Eduardo Pondal

There were three hundred crows combed by the wind.

And there was a girl and a church.

One day, the girl, who always used to play in the vicinity, noticed that all the animals and trees had gone quiet. Not only that, they were listening intently, the crows suspended like brushstrokes in the pollen of a rarefied shining.

The light suddenly diminished and a storm charged out of the void of the Outer Sea, making the whole sky above Nemancos shatter into a thousand pieces.

The girl, holding against her breast a baby boy, in reality a dog with a harlequin's patches, sought shelter in the porch, where she knew of the company of the orchestra of elderly musicians and of a smiling prophet in stone. There was also a coarsely worked skull, however, which peered at her that day through the dark holes of its eyes. So the girl pushed open the creaking door and entered the church, in which the nave was separated from the aisles by tall pillars, and which, empty as it was, resembled the hall of a huge palace, long since protected from intruders.

She crossed herself, and the dog, at the font and sat huddled in one of the pews at the back, near a Virgin Mary of sorrowful countenance, dressed in a mantle of black mourning, and her bared heart pierced by seven swords.

Girl and virgin viewed each other sorrowfully, because by now the thunder resounded angrily and rolled furiously across the tiles. The little girl began to think that the storm's cart had come to a halt right there, on top of the church, and that it was after her, and had something inside it, a fathomless hollow, which at times gnawed at her stomach and moaned through the dog's throat. So she decided to go and see if there was somebody in the vestry; she hoped it might be her mother, who arranged the flowers and lit the candles. But just as she was making her way there, a bolt of lightning crashed into the belfry and flashed against the metal structure. The thunder rang out so loud that the stone's innards trembled. The girl was so afraid that she could not move her legs and she leant against the whitewashed wall and closed her eyes to see if that would make the storm go away.

With the din some distance off, having faded into a trot as it disappeared down the celestial corridor that leads to Compostela, the girl came out of her shell in search of air and light and, on doing so, noticed flecks of dust on her eyelashes and lips, and then saw how round about her the whitewash had fallen over wood and stone, and was scattered in large scabs and small flakes.

She then heard an uproar of people, accompanied by titters and swishing skirts, so she turned towards the wall, and seeing what she saw, the body, round about the height of the abdomen, she would have shrunk back into her shell, but her eyes refused to obey her, rather they opened wider of their own accord and ran from one end to the other, as if on a rail, and then round and round, as if drawing a figure of eight. The girl managed to avert them for a moment to see what the virgins were saying, but the images filled her with wonder in a way they had never done before.

The old wall was now alive with colour. And when she was able finally to control her eyes, the girl saw that the colours were forms and the forms were people, individuals and animals that drew the light and cast a shadow over all the rest. Blinded by what was too much for her, she stepped backwards and climbed up on to a pew.

And from there, at the level of her eyes – to go into further detail – she came across a bird of prey with a woman's head, which rather than frightening her struck her as quite funny. What caused her most delight, however, were the ladies, most of whom were out of story-books: they were beautiful, dressed as queens, and so elegant that gold thread showed along the edges and lace butterflies bordering the velvet and silver filaments in the hairnets, not to mention the glow of the gems and the precious glint of the stones in the jewels. She was very amused that one of the beautiful ladies should be riding a ram, and even more that a devil in the scene, peeping out from behind the curtains in carnival fashion, was holding a trident at the ready.

The girl then heard some voices that came not from the fantasy but from the porch, calling for her, and sounding like her mother, who now appeared in the doorway between the sun's beams that rise up after the storm with musical warbles to pinch the startled skin of the earth. She was holding a real baby Jesus in her arms, wrapped in her shawl, and only she knew how much he weighed, having carried him all over the village in search of her daughter once she had seen what it was the bolt of lightning had in mind. All the anguish in her eyes was on account of the girl with the plaits who, thanks be to God, was leaping about the church and who, thanks be to God again, was going to get a hiding, from which only a miracle could save her.

"Look, Mummy, there are saints everywhere!"

The mother crossed herself upon the first impression, and fell down on her knees, seeing – it was true – only female saints richly dressed, without observing at first that one of them was pregnant, another brazenly exposing her breast, another holding up a sucking-pig on a spit, to say nothing of the harpy and the one riding a ram. In response to the shouts of the mother, who had left the church and run down the narrow streets spreading the news about the miracle of Arán, the locals gathered immediately, two score neighbours, though once upon a time there had been more, enough to support a manor and a monastery with abbot. Of the powers of yesteryear all that remained was a cassock belonging to Don Xil, who was related to the local gentry, and who – getting back to the story – was the last to find out, having been out hunting an elusive hare that had bewitched him. When he returned to the rectory, a little crestfallen, the defeated dog panting at his heels, he noticed with some surprise that the doors of the church were wide open and that inside candles were lit. The priest hurried along, fearing some damage on account of the storm, which had caught them out in the fields and dampened their spirits, forcing them to seek shelter in a mill from which they were able to watch the hare take immaculate flight, wrapped in a luminous halo, until it disappeared into the shady green of the alders.

What the priest encountered inside the temple were lots of people conversing in the half-light. Since no one seemed to realize that he had arrived, dark as he was, and despite the iron on his boots which echoed on the flagstones, he let loose a few customary cries, but was soon dazzled by the glow of all the candles burning next to the altar of Our Lady of Sorrows.

"You should know," said the priest in Sunday's sermon, "that these women are not saints but sinners. Worse than that, they are the deceptive illustration of evil, the very sins themselves. These ladies of beautiful aspect, who beguile our eyes if we are not forewarned, are in fact temptations of blackened soul, the heralds of hell, the seven heads of a single serpent."

The church was full, brimming with people as on one of Our Lady's feastdays or on All Souls' Day. Many had come in from neighbouring parts to view these ladies of Arán who had flowered on the wall and had been given the name – with not a great deal of accuracy, so it seemed – of the Saintly Figures. The priest had spent three days and three nights preparing the homily, as was evident from the bags under his eyes, despite his ruddy complexion, for something within told him that his office was being put to the test and matters needed to be taken in hand. And although the hare would from time to time cross between the sepia lines of the *Relief for Parish Priests*, or *Informal Sermons for Use with Congregations*, he had worked conscientiously on the homily, and even rehearsed the contours of his speech and his gestures, for he had not practised in a long time, the sacred words had grown mouldy in a corner of the attic, the years had brought about a certain loss of appetite, he was weighed down by the fatal muteness with which the facts of life revealed themselves, tortured by being confined to the animal kingdom, by the weaknesses that appeared now in angelic form, since down the channel of letters the girl with plaits ran as well, the one sitting right there, opposite the pulpit, wearing a blue dress with white motifs, and with large, jet-black eyes that had a way of looking straight through things.

"The one you see down there at the end," said Don Xil, pointing an accusatory finger, "who with an innocent air and great charm holds an ilex branch in her left hand, and with her right hand proffers an acorn to the pig, that one, whose back is protected by a knight in a cuirass of steel plates, that is none other than Covetousness, the most voracious of the roots of evil. You'll see that the pig raises its snout towards its lady, because after one acorn it wants another, and when there are no longer any left, it'll dig in the ground, because this is what covetousness does to those who become possessed by it, they want everything, both what is theirs and what isn't, and they don't stop scheming until they get it. The pig, the knight in the cuirass and the lady are one and the same person, but it is the woman who embodies the sin.

"Nor should you look too favourably on the one next to her, this one who is so haughty, crowned, dressed in red and of noble appearance, for she is none other than Pride, holding a mirror in one hand and a turkey in the other. Such a conspicuous colour will not fool anyone who is suitably prepared. Red is the fire of hell and clothed in red with choleric blood is he who oversees its ovens, for it is Lucifer who directs the whole operation, on the lookout for unsuspecting souls, sticking out his tongue at all of us.

"They are all related, but the next one is more closely linked to the first and is called Avarice. Her stomach is swollen, as if she were pregnant, but what she carries inside her is not a healthy creature but the repulsive fruit of avidity, in the manner of leeches, those voracious worms that fill the jar she holds in her hand.

"You can see how deceptive these figures really are, for that pleasant-looking lady with rosy cheeks and flowing black locks, that is none other than Ire. Persons of this nature, who are swift to react, will quickly lay hand to arms, and there she is with the sword unsheathed, holding in the other hand a burning torch which is giving off smoke, hence the saying *Fumantem viri nasum ne tetigeris*, or, 'Don't touch the nose of a man who is fuming'."

At this point, Don Xil made a pause, allowing the chords of Latin to vibrate. And he concluded that they were following the homily most attentively, because they would all in unison turn their heads to him after observing each of the paintings in the fresco, though perhaps they were adopting a different perspective and sought the smoke blowing from his own nostrils, the colour rising to his own cheeks, since the priest was well known for possessing, among other attributes, a very fiery temper.

And since everyone, deep down, is aware of their own faults and which foot is lame, so to speak, he concentrated somewhat more forcibly on the following lady, the one riding high on the back of the ram and stroking a partridge, who was now the centre of attention and demanded a censure suitable for such a challenge. Don Xil thought that God was truly fearsome indeed and manipulated the human threads implacably. Everything that was happening could only be understood as an unequivocal warning that he was in the divine line of fire, and this terrified him, because his faith, and there was no doubting the sincerity of it, was not the intuitive, sentimental faith of innocents, which he envied so much and which, deep down, irritated him, but the absolute certainty that God existed, that in effect He was omnipotent and that His patience had a limit. This was not something that he could freely proclaim, but the best way to get on with God was to escape His notice, and the worst thing that could happen – as when a lord fixes his gaze on a serf who is minding his own business or a human observes the presence of an insect clambering up his thumb – the worst thing was if the Almighty for some reason should latch on to him, locate him in the remote village lost in time with His infinite magnifying glass.

7

Release me, God, release me!

But this is not what he shouted. Instead, with accusing finger, he pointed to the girl with curly locks, stroking her partridge and riding what she was riding. "Lust!" And he noticed how they read his lips, hearing one thing, but listening to another, and he counted up to ten, slowly, lest any of them should forget that above all things, far above the marshy ground upon which they stood, he was who he was. He was the Word, the Voice from Beyond. He lost his fear of all of them, of the girl's look as well. "This one, wearing no more than a cloth to cover her private parts, plays maid to the Devil, works for him at all hours, and the fruit of her fleeting joy is merely perdition. She makes the virtuous man repugnant and turns the master into a slave, she ruins earthly goods and keeps us from heaven. She knows how to ride a ram, we can see that, which is the form of unrestrained appetite for unclean acts, for you'll no doubt realize that these paintings, which in ancient times were referred to as allegories, show what they want to without actually showing it. So, if this creature with curly locks is stroking the partridge, don't think the gesture is an innocent one. Anyone familiar with the workings of the animal kingdom, and there are expert hunters among you," he said with modesty, "will not be unaware of this bird's insatiable desire, and the male's capacity to drag the female with him and destroy the clutch in savage intercourse."

It was a lot of people for so much silence and the rector, gazing upon them, thought that perhaps he had surpassed himself in the details, he could feel what seemed like wheels on his tongue, which had a life of its own, as must the hand of the anonymous rogue who had painted the ancient fresco, embellishing the vices on the pretext of fighting them and filling the heads of the uncultured with lewd images, for how impotent words can be compared to colours, that explosive combination of silent temptations and burning anathema, and who could resist on arriving home and finding themselves alone, male and female, flesh against flesh, with Curly Locks galloping in the memory astride the beast, and stroking the partridge. He himself, with his innards in turmoil, could feel the salty taste of the skin of nostalgia on the tip of his tongue, he relived the scenes of the fall as if they were the decisive moment of existence, and realized – it was only a happy and painful glimmer like a flash that reaches the eyes – that the girl, that forbidden girl, wretched flower, sown in another's field, had been his sole work, the single trace on a road without return.

"This other lady with the elongated neck like the bird which is known as a crane, holding a sucking-pig on a spit, needless to say this is Gluttony, which is the sin of eating all things to excess, for there are people whose whole being revolves around the dinner table. The reason the neck is so long and thin, in contrast to the bloated shape of the belly, is so that it can better enjoy its food. And then there is one whose face is more drawn and emaciated, carrying a heart in her hands. Don't be fooled into thinking that this is some kind of penance or love pang. The heart is her own and she is about to sink her teeth in, such is Envy, who suffers on account of the good or prosperity of others. Pay particular attention to her hair. Snakes intertwined in representation of evil thoughts!

"And the only lady left is the one in the coffin. The end of the passage. Death, that skeleton which at the end of the wall draws the bow and forgives no one. There, where true life begins for the blessed, for sinners is the start of an appalling journey, because that poisoned arrow plunges them into the stinking pit where there are no colours, except for the tongues of burning tar.

"I am well aware," said the minister, now in a deeper voice, and the parishioners knew that it was in confidence, "I am well aware that at this crossroads friends and favours count for nothing and one never knows when the pitcher is full. For a mere peccadillo a friend can go to Hell, because it's the least fervent who most annoy God, and, just as the Lord has our days numbered, so He has counted up the sins

He is going to allow us; for some that's two, for others ten, for others a hundred. But how do we know? The inhabitants of Sodom were allowed many, great sins before He lost His patience, whereas the people of Damascus were only allowed three. God took away the life of Moses, with whom He had a close relationship, in the desert for a single offence and forbad him to enter the Promised Land. For a venial sin committed by David, the Lord sent him a plague that lasted three days and killed 70,000."

And even when they were saying Amen, they all thought that was a lot of dead for a trifling thing, except for Rosa, the girl with the plaits, who was counting on her fingers and could not take her eyes off the skeleton, for she would have sworn that the day of discovery was somewhere else.

3

"And it turned out that the last king of Galicia was taken prisoner by his brother Don Alfonso, king of León, and lived in captivity until his death in Castillo de Luna, eighteen years with chains around his ankles, and this is how he asked to be buried in Terra de Foris, in fetters as he had lived.

"And that is why he lives now in the woods, up in the Pena Forcada range, where he's been spotted between Canladrón and Home do Lazo, a white crow with silver chains and a ball of jet.

"And all those you can see," said the lady, pointing abruptly towards the window, in which the fields were visible outside, "all those flying against the wind, are his warriors. The 300 crows of Xallas!"

"Crows bring bad luck," said Rosa from the sink. She had her sleeves rolled up and her hands had grown purple under the cold tap. But she in turn looked out of the window, which let in the porcelain light.

"What do you mean, bad luck!" the lady said with a smile that was stuck to her and to which the wrinkles had moulded themselves as if the skin were guided by a sweet determination. "Did you know? Crows kept the saints in the mountains alive with bread. They would take Saint Anthony a crust in their beaks."

"I once . . ." said the elder boy, opening his eyes wide as if recollecting a dream, ". . . saw a crow eating a bag of crisps."

"What flavour were they?" asked the girl, nudging him.

"Cheese and onion."

"I don't like cheese and onion," said the girl.

"Nor do I," the boy continued. "The crow was up on the roof, next to the chimney, and opened the bag with its beak, like this, it was very clever, holding on to it with its feet. Then it took out the crisps one by one."

"Aargh! They taste horrible!" said the girl. "And they make your tongue sting."

"Well, it liked them."

"In truth they were not warriors," the lady took up the thread. "The king of Galicia was not very keen on the sword. He was friends with the Moorish king of Seville, and also with the Norman king to the north. This king was the father of an extremely beautiful princess, who was very fair and had such pale skin that when she drank red wine you could see it running down her throat. She was to have married the king of Galicia. But he was taken prisoner and the Norman king died before he could come to the aid of his Galician friend."

"What did he die of?" asked the boy.

"I think he fell off his horse," said the lady. "Sometimes kings die like that."

At this point, Simón, who had been half asleep at the end of the table, his head against the wall, with his mouth ajar and his eyes closed, came to in a state of consternation and looked anxiously round about.

"If they were not warriors, what were they then?" asked the boy once again, intrigued.

"Poets," the lady said, continuing to watch the sluggish flight of the birds into the wind, which looked as if they were trying to pass through an invisible pane of glass. "The king of Galicia had an army of troubadours, equipped with harps, zithers and hurdy-gurdies."

"I heard tell," came Rosa's voice from the sink, where she was washing up a zinc pot, "I heard tell that the crows were also the victims of a great famine that occurred."

"There was a great famine," said the lady, "the result of a potato blight. People had to eat grass, and farmhands came to die in the streets of the cities. They were dirty and dressed in rags, knocking in vain at street doors. The stronger ones killed themselves, rather than suffer the indignity of begging. Some hanged themselves from apple trees at dawn. Many others left for America, piled up in the holds of boats, like slaves."

"All that happened here?" the boy asked.

The girl had gone outside and came racing back in.

"It's true, there is a crow!" she shouted. "It's on the chimney."

There was, of course. It was on the chimney-top, keeping watch, in the service of the king of Galicia.

Rosa then called for silence, turned off the tap and listened carefully. She dried her hands on the apron.

"It's the baby," she said in a resigned tone. "The baby's crying and dinner's not ready. What a night awaits me!"

4

When night fell, not covering everything, but opening the celestial book with twelve plates, the signs of the zodiac, the house crow took to the air, its hood drenched, and went to report to the king of Galicia.

"The fat man," Toimil announced in a disparaging tone, "came whizzing up in his car and, when he got out, I think he was reeling, but he pulled himself together and entered the house making a real racket. The baby, whom the mother had just managed to settle down, started crying again. And when he carried on shouting, Rosa shouted as well."

"And what about the lady?"

"The lady had disappeared into the darkness. Simón showed her the way.

"It would seem there were two glasses of Oporto wine on the table and some salted biscuits in the shape of fish and this clearly annoyed him more, because he said that was quite enough of such treatment, the old lady was, was . . . but he didn't get any further, because Rosa sent the children to bed, and told them to put on their pyjamas and say their prayers."

"I come in and I'm treated like a dog!" said the husband.

"Don't talk like that in front of the children!"

"I'll talk how I damn well like. This is my house!"

"You've been drinking!"

"Don't make me angry!"

"I can smell it in the air," said Rosa, pressing her cheek to that of the baby she rocked in her arms. "Do you think I can't tell?"

"Of course I've been drinking!" he growled, downing one of the glasses. "But the smell was already here. So the old vixen likes her sweet wine, does she?"

Rosa waited for the child in her arms to stop sobbing, sat down and covered him with her shawl. Her husband drew near to the fire, rubbed his hands and then shoved a log with his boot until the part that was red-hot disintegrated into embers.

"She came to keep me company. She kept the kids amused."

"She's like a witch!"

"Don't talk nonsense."

"She's got you under her spell!"

Rosa was silent for a moment, as if confirming the spell. She stared absent-mindedly at her husband's boot as he stamped on the log.

Finally she said calmly, as if thinking about the other gave her some comfort, "She never has a bad word to say about anyone. It's as if she's from another world. She's always so happy!"

"Who wouldn't be?" the husband shouted, suddenly turning to face his wife. "I'd be in heaven as well! With others to look after me . . ."

"But, Cholo, she hardly eats a thing. She nibbles at a bit of lettuce and then asks for some herbal tea."

". . . and a domestic who comes free of charge."

"I go when I want to. No one forces me."

"That's right! And meanwhile here the dinner's not made."

Rosa got up angrily. She proceeded to the far end of the kitchen, opened the pantry and returned, the child in one arm, with a plate full of bacon, cabbage and boiled potatoes.

"There you are!"

"Don't throw the plate at me like I'm a pig!"

The baby burst out crying again. She carried him upstairs.

"You never used to think like that," she remarked from the landing.

"Didn't I?" her husband murmured, perched over his plate.

"None of you used to think like that. The rich woman was coming! The rich woman was coming! That's all you used to say!"

"Women!" the husband sighed to himself. He had pulled out a small wad of notes held together by an elastic band and was counting them. He put them away and began eating hungrily. Upstairs the children were running around, spurred on by bitter commands.

"What are you doing watching television?" Rosa was shouting. "Haven't I told you to go to bed? All day long watching rubbish!"

"Women!" he repeated. He knew how to calm her, randy as she was. In an hour, he would be riding her and she would be moaning, stuck to his body, surrendered, under control.

"Look at that, Toimil," said the king of Galicia, reading the starry night with melancholy. "The Sun has risen as high as the Goat, and the sky has got its golden buskins on. And here we are, watching it all from the ashes of a faded star, slaves of a nightmare they call History. The world is frozen, Toimil!"

"It must be my rheumatism," said the house crow, "but I have to confess this winter's getting on my nerves. If you don't mind me saying so, my lord, what wouldn't I give to taste a red Amandi wine out of a Buño jar!"

5

Rosa was on the trail of a mouse. It horrified her to think of it in the house, touching and sniffing at everything. The kitchen was like a paten, not a speck of dirt in the corners or underneath the furniture; she had washed the floor using bleach and polished it. She had also put out air fresheners with a lemon fragrance. She had wrapped all the edibles that were not in the fridge in white cloths and aluminium foil, not just the soft items, but whatever came in a box or tin, like the María Fontaneda biscuits and La Onza de Oro sardines, such was the war she was waging. And before she went to bed, dreading that it might explore the landscape of the plates and dishes, which, without her knowledge, told the story of a Chinese princess who ran off with her forbidden lover, and turned into a turtledove, she covered the crockery with a tablecloth.

All she would leave, right in the middle of the marble work surface, was a trap with a small piece of cheese as bait.

When she woke up, she would lie in bed awhile, waiting for her husband to go down first, afraid to see what she had already pictured in her mind's eye: the body crushed by the iron spring. In fact she would open her eyes, thinking that she had heard the noise of the trap. But every morning she would find the device intact, except for the bait, which had disappeared, the hook of the trap licked clean. The local cheese being very soft, she bought a cube of Manchego cheese, which she did not like, because it was too hard, but the mouse scoffed all of that as well in small helpings. Rosa then left it some chorizo, securing the sausage by the fat, shortening the distance of the mechanism that sprang loose and activated the trap as far as it would go, and she poured some drops of oil to make it more slippery, playing around with it in the air so much she was afraid she might get her own hand caught. But the devil of a rodent refused to be taken in and caused her husband to laugh at her as he went out the front door. Rosa would imagine it emerging from some hole – she had inspected the whole kitchen without finding anything that could be the mouth of a burrow, the slightest refuge for a fistful of shade, there were cracks at the end of the skirting boards, but they were for ants, and she had poked into everything without encountering a single soul except for some sleepy spiders, but the mouse had to be coming from somewhere – and she would see it peeping out with a crafty smile, a glint in its eyes, to survey the woman's territory as if in vivid caricature of a cruel strip cartoon, because it had no doubt who its enemy was, whom it disgusted, who prepared the trap each night with nervous hands. It could not fail to detect her scent, the woman's scent, on the bait and on the trap, on the edibles, on the blue landscape of the crockery, and throughout the room where she was the only one not just passing through and where she reigned in the manner of a domestic.

One Friday, as a test, she put out some fresh fish, with the skin tightly fastened to the spring. The following morning, she found it just as she had left it. The mouse, it would seem, was a picky eater. "At least you'll go hungry today, you rascal!" But then she saw by the droppings that it had been on the bench by the hearth and something told her to open the newspaper that was lying there, in which she found half the obituary page had been gnawed away.

And so it was that the story of the mouse became for Rosa a nightmare that she recounted to no-one. She listened to silences, saw nothings. And she turned it over in her mind so much that – to avoid having nothing to say, not even "yes, I've mice in the house like everyone else" – she took advantage of a trip to Coruña to buy some poison. It was a cardboard box with a red background and a black silhouette that resembled a rat more than a mouse, and on which, on arriving home, she read, holding it with the tips of her fingers at a short distance: *Racumín, rat poison for guest rodents*. And then, underlined: <u>*A single mouthful will suffice*</u>. She put on some orange rubber gloves, opened the box and saw that it contained some silver sachets which she could not tear by hand. So she went upstairs to find some scissors. And it occurred to her that, while she was upstairs, the wretched mouse had emerged from its hole and, with some reading glasses it had, was spelling out the formula: *sul fa qui no xa . . . line*. When she found what she needed, she raced down the stairs to see if she might catch it unawares. But the mouse had already retreated to its burrow. Rosa picked up the box, glanced again at the caption, briefly noticing the word *mouthful*, and cut off the corner of not just one, nor two, but all ten sachets in the box, laying them out in each corner of the kitchen. She told Simón not to let a single cat or dog into the house and the elder children, who were a boy and a girl, not to touch anything in there and not to play in that part of the house. But the boy, not hearing her very well, approached one of the corners and asked, "What's that, Mum, that's so pretty in its silver foil?" and she smacked him hard across the face, "Don't look at it, you hear, don't even look at it!" And he turned around without crying, his face all red, in such a way that he seemed to be saying, "You're mad, Mum, mad." And that made her even more nervous and she bundled them upstairs. At night, when she went to the bathroom, she looked at herself in the mirror before going to bed and saw large bags under her eyes and felt so tired that she thought she was going to be ill. Once in bed, she collapsed exhausted, with the baby next to her, not bothering to put him in the cradle. When her husband came back home, late, he must have noticed something, because he turned over, letting an arm drop to the ground.

The following morning, the woman examined each of the small piles of pink granules of Racumín poison in their silver foil. It was obvious that no-one had tasted them, that nothing had been nibbled or spread about, but in the hope that it might eat a mouthful, even if it were only one, she left them until Sunday, because that day she did not want poison in the house. And she waited. To tell the truth, she was rushed off her feet all day long, but she kept a sharp lookout in case she should come across the furry body at last, stiff, with its feet in the air. She had heard that mice, when they have a presage of death by poison, emerge from their burrows in broad daylight, stagger about as if searching for something, paying no attention to people, and collapse in an open space right in the middle of the kitchen.

But nothing happened and the bags under Rosa's eyes turned violet, and she became so anxious that she lost her appetite and the little sense of humour she had left. This had a marked effect on the others, because Simón, who was her brother, and who had never uttered a word on account of something that happened to him as a child, a melancholic air, it was said, due to lying down in an empty grave inside the cemetery, well, this Simón, whenever he was in the house, would spend the day shut up in his room, listening to Mexican *corridos* and *rancheras*, folk songs he liked a lot, just as he liked horses (you only had to see his face when he got on one, it made you want to cry seeing him there, like a king).

And during that time she stopped visiting Misia, the lady who had returned to the old manor house. Misia noticed that something was amiss but was not surprised, everybody had ended up moving away from her since the day she had turned up without a husband or treasure and with those strange habits, such as eating only vegetables and going for cycle rides along the cart-tracks, in trousers or with her skirts tucked up, wearing a harvester's hat, straw with a black ribbon, with all the charm of a young lady's picture hat. And what set the tongues wagging even further was that she had spent all she seemed to own on a flock of sheep, which roamed freely, until night-time, when she would round them up and let them into the house through the front door.

Rosa's greatest desire was to catch the mouse before it was Christmas.

Until one day, on the eve, she saw it.

And the mouse saw her.

Rosa was standing next to the table, peeling fruit for the baby's food, when her eyes were drawn towards the kitchen work surface, and it took her a while to realize that, in effect, what they were looking at, to the point of being able to count the hairs in its moustache, what stood watching her in its turn, was the selfsame mouse. To her own surprise, she neither panicked nor shouted. She remained calm, slicing the banana now, one eye here and the other on the little fellow. Next, with a control that simply amazed her, she began to crush the fruit with a fork. And when she had finished making up the dish it occurred to her to taste it, not in the way she normally did, quickly and without thinking, but slowly, licking her lips right in the intruder's face. It was then that it turned around and began walking and, as relaxed as can be, started climbing up the gas pipe. It then became obvious that it was not thin but fat, with a disproportionately large bum. When it reached the lower platform of the gas heater, instead of disappearing in a trice, it proceeded to make itself comfortable and looked out again to see if she was still eating. But Rosa had lost her previous sense of peace by now and was beside herself, running with the knife in her hand, shouting, "Pig! Swine! Bastard! Wretch!" and she stuck the point of the knife in amongst the iron without feeling anything that was not metal. She put the knife down and with an icy glare pressed the automatic lighter and turned the gas dial round to full, causing a large flame to spring up. She would have liked it very much, at that moment, if the stink of gas had been of skin and charred flesh as well.

But the mouse returned the following day, when it was time to prepare the baby's food. On this occasion, the woman compulsively threw the plate against the shelf where it was walking, the fruit went all over the wall, but even so the mouse made little haste, picking its way through the broken pieces of china, forced to take flight but unwillingly; how sorry it seemed not to have a taste of the baby's pudding. Again it went back the way it had come, dragging its bum behind it, its tail hanging listlessly as if it had one just for the sake of it.

Rosa turned on the heater, more than anything to give herself a rest, with little hope of frightening the glutton. On reflection, however, she turned the whole thing off and started to dismantle the bodywork. At first she could see nothing that might give shelter in that iron maze. But just as she was about to put it back together, she noticed that the plate holding the apparatus to the wall had some holes, and that one of them, rather than revealing the white of the wall, was dark, so she poked in it with a stick and discovered that it was deep but the stick could not go along it because the hole curved at the end. The woman started thinking as she cleared up the mess. And without paying attention to the baby, who was calling for his food, she went to the barn and got some handfuls of cement from a sack that her husband kept there, and prepared it without sand, using a small amount of water, because she thought it would be more resistant like that, and began packing it into the hole.

This operation, the fact of having taken the initiative, calmed her raging spirits, and after several days of anxiety, she was able to sleep peacefully.

And now that she was feeling somewhat stronger, early the following morning she was the first to go downstairs and saw, with relief, that nobody had disturbed her work, nor did she take much notice of what her husband said to her, laughing as he spoke, about mice preferring to nibble at dried cement. Unfortunately for her, this time he was not lying, and the following day, at teatime, Rosa saw it climbing down the pipe; something had told her it was there, and without thinking twice about it, overcoming the desire she had to cry, she let it go no further and banged with her fist against the bodywork of the heater and then put her own fingers in the hole, scratching furiously at the cement.

Later, while squashing the fruit and cleaning it by removing the skin and solids, she thought of the most terrible thing that could possibly happen to a throat. She made up her mind and returned to the barn for some more cement. Back in the house, she spread a plastic sheet on the ground and broke a glass bottle on it, smashing all the pieces with a hammer until they were really small, like sharp needles. Then she took all the pins out of the sewing box and added them to the mass. With the greatest care, she placed the prickly paste in the crumbling hole, pushing it and cramming it with the head of a chisel, but even so she accidentally cut her fingertip and licked what is known as a trickle of blood but which in her case was a petal.

And that sacrificial blood told her that this time she had conquered the nightmare.

6

When the mouse had bored its way outside through a join between the stones, involving a great deal of effort on its part and with a pin sticking out of its snout, having climbed down a tendril of ivy, it did not like being out in the open at all, for the cold took its breath away, and it decided to go back in through the front door like a gentleman and tell her, should it be necessary, for once breaking the rules of those who are on the other side, that the house belonged to the two of them just the same.

But as it was ruminating thus, it was met by the crow, who looked very imposing in that hood and bespeckled black smock.

"Whither goest thou, Xil de Arán?" exclaimed the crow with great authority, in a tone that sounded more like a warning than a question.

"What's it to you, if you don't mind me asking?" replied the minister, really quite annoyed at having been recognized.

"One more step, Don Xil, and I'll take you prisoner!"

"A little quiet and peace," said the mouse, somewhat muddled by the fear he felt, and not knowing how to face up to such an unexpected turn of events. Then he remembered the Latin of yesteryear and with it the power of tonic conjuration in order to assert himself. "*Elephantem ex musca facere!*"

"Stop bothering her, Don Xil, that's quite enough," said the crow, unimpressed.

"I don't know what you mean."

"And the causes of all mortals from Adam to the last that is born in this world will be read aloud. And the books of consciences that were closed in each lifetime will be opened. That'll do for now."

"Well, you're not Saint John," said the mouse finally, in a daze. "Who are you then?"

"Toimil of Bergantiños, protonotary to the king of Galicia!" the crow introduced himself, and did so with solemnity, not to appear vain but to show that he had been taught good manners.

"In that case, since we're both important people, supposing we come to some kind of agreement?" Don Xil retorted, catching his breath, and finding the office somewhat fantastical, knowing, furthermore, being well read as he was, that there were no other kings than those of Spain.

"You see that light that's just gone on?" said Toimil, on the verge of losing his patience. "Life has returned to the manor house. Your place is there, not among the lives of the tenants."

"But my heart draws me to this house!" exclaimed Don Xil, wearing a hurt expression, which he may not have been putting on.

Toimil was about to point out that what he meant by "heart" was in fact food, but he kept quiet because he was as refined as he was upright. What he did say was that the mandate was final and that the mouse should procure lodgings in the manor house, which should not be too difficult for him since he knew it like the back of his hand, from the bread oven to the attic, not forgetting the granaries and the dovecote which had a sailing ship for a weather-vane. He also said that he would have plenty to nibble at, since things were up and running again. If he did not comply, the king of Galicia's army would put him in his place.

"I see no such armada," said Don Xil humorously and to find out if there was one.

"All those you can see," responded Toimil, pointing very seriously to his look-alikes that were forever jousting with the wind, "are the 300 crows of Xallas! Among them are twelve hidalgos who've been ordered by the king to keep a special eye on you. They're holding you in custody, Xil!"

The old pater followed the crows' acrobatic manoeuvres with attention. They had been there all his life, roving the landscape like a flock of ragged, starving tramps. He had never noticed anything noble about them, anything distinctive in their shabby flight. But now, as he watched them closely, that same sluggishness transformed into a heraldic heaviness, as if their flying were a kind of laborious handwriting on the parchment of time. The signs they traced with stubborn determination gave the landscape a certain gravity. If they were not there, he thought, Arán would make for a more trivial stage set. It would be impossible to perform the important matter of insoluble tragedy.

"From the earthly point of view, such an arrangement strikes me as arbitrary," he said finally in a resigned tone, convinced now of the seriousness of the situation. "I do not think it is right for the king to govern sentiment."

This is the kingdom that awaits us, thought Toimil. The king of Galicia is a poor king of hearts. But the protonotary spoke without ceremony.

"It's the manor house or hell!" Toimil shouted, firmly pointing his black wing in the direction of the large house that stood atop the hill, printed on a romantic dusky indigo blue.

7

As tawny night fell, when the tired village lineages collapsed in front of the television, the lady would delight in undressing in her bedroom next to a stoked brazier in the hope of warming her feet one day, wearing as she did in winter tights and three pairs of socks, though still the blood did not reach her toes, which had nothing to do with old age, since even when she was a child, before going to bed, they would wash them in hot water without it ever scalding, and then they would iron her sheets, but when she woke up, she could no longer feel her feet on account of the cold and they would have to massage them for the colour to come back, so that she could stand on them. It was a family failing; otherwise she preferred to dress lightly and relished the pleasure she felt now, the wolf of night coldly licking her back, the tender tongues of heat crawling up her front, slowly, entwining her thighs like ardent ivy and, pushing up from the hips, encircling her breasts, brushing against them with their lips until they grow firm, not as before but taking their time, like a lotus or a camellia, and then adhering to the neck and kissing her whole face, first softly, then passionately, the fingers of the fire caught up in her flowing hair, holding on to it, interlocking at the back of her neck, as she bends down towards her lover, rotating her head with her eyes closed. And when she turned around, all of a sudden, she put her hands back on her knees and doubled over in such a way that the sheets of gold leaf shimmered on her buttocks. But it was over in the twinkle of an eye, because now, as if she had lost the thread of a dream, she stretches and shakes her head, at the same time running her fingers through her hair, and very quickly, seeing the cold baring its teeth, puts on some flannel pyjamas which to Don Xil de Arán looked as if they were men's pyjamas, though he was unable to give the matter a great deal of thought because at that moment the lady went up to the dressing table and turned on a lamp.

The sudden gleam of light stunned him and Don Xil, instead of escaping back the way he had come, remained huddled against the base of the mirror, frosted with swans all around the edge, directly behind a cardboard box on which was a beautiful woman with a pierced nose, who might well have been called Nostalgia, judging by her expression, but what it said on the box was Henna of Pakistan, concealed from the lady's sight, for the moment, by a jar on which he read The Body Shop, and below that Against animal testing. The woman's fingers danced and felt around the area, finally spotting the tweezers. And Don Xil was able to subdue the fear that glinted in his eyes, since time came to a standstill or proceeded very slowly along the grey eyebrows of the woman sitting at the mirror. His insides were churned up not only as a result of the sudden light, but also by the recent memory of his naked niece, her body faintly illuminated by the glow of the coals bathing her skin like a stained glass window warmed by the setting sun and, most of all, the revelation of that body which in old age was like a lily, so soft and hard at once it seemed, for this is the mysterious way in which time sometimes pauses. Don Xil was amazed now, as he stuck out his snout incautiously, by the grace with which she coiled her hair into a bun and then combed it till her locks were long and smooth, shiny all over, and by the way in which she put back the curls using only her curved fingers. When she seemed satisfied, the lady licked her lips and bit them, and then pressed one against the other. Still watching herself, the image reflected back at her with the melancholic smile that family mirrors retain, Misia opened the drawer of the dressing table and her hands took out a jewel which, when she put it around her neck, was shown to consist of holly leaves with jet berries mounted in the old style. And this is how Don Xil saw all the women who walked along the corridors of the manor house or whiled away the hours in the sun lounge, among begonias and miniature roses, as the rain fell on the skin of the world. A knot stuck in the transmigrator's throat because everything that had fallen apart shone now in her, rising victorious above the ruins, finally recognized by the mirror. While time stopped for her, as she played like a little girl with earrings and rings that she modelled on the fan of her hand, the other one present sank into nostalgia and calculation, for while it was true that her face conjured up a thousand memories and a bitter delight, it was no less certain that he was at a loss what to make of the exhibition of family treasures that he supposed had been discreetly pawned or mislaid in the maze of inheritance. Among them was a brooch that a member of the house of Arán, the sinner Don Álvaro Mosquera, this Xil's great uncle, had brought back from Brazil, a jewel with a mysterious stone set in it cut in the shape of a heart, which throbbed in the light, the pulsations visible in the gleam of an artefact whose origin was never fully established, since the adventurer had a different story each day, it had come from the hands of a prospector in exchange for a pistol or from an Indian in return for a tinder-box, until he began to distance himself and not to want to talk about the stone, as if he were afraid of it, and it was precisely this brooch that Misia placed now in the hollow of her breasts to fasten the top of her pyjamas; it was a whimsical way to go to sleep, the madder branch of the family had these strange habits, but then, who knows, perhaps she did wisely at a time when thieves were on the trail of burglars, since a woman's cleavage has never been a bad place to hide things. When she turned out the lamp, her eyes and the heart made of precious stone continued to sparkle in the velvet night.

Don Xil slipped down the gap between the wall and the table and on reaching the ground, with the lady under the canopy delivered into the arms of Morpheus, he turned his attention to other matters, for he could feel the anxiety in his teeth and a hole in his stomach as if he had been fasting. He had come to the bedroom in the wake of people, for where there are people there are crumbs, but his niece had never eaten much and now, it seemed, she lived off the air. Shelves, cupboard and trough were all empty, the only food in the kitchen was a still life with a hare and a red partridge hanging on the wall, which mortified Don Xil; at least it might have been on the ground so that he could have fed the illusion on paint. There was nothing for it but to dine on paper, and there was not even much of that, only two books remained in what had been the great library of Arán manor: the *Relief for Parish Priests* and a small, well-thumbed manual, *The Liberal Ways of Hunting*. He had sold all the rest to an antique dealer by the pound, damaged as they were by the damp and mould; books also need a pat on the back from time to time, and it was a shame to let them go to waste and not to plan ahead. This left him with the terrible dilemma of choosing between devotion and duty for a bite to eat. He was still pondering the problem as he followed the skirting boards towards the library when he was alerted by a noise that had become familiar recently and was none other than a mouse's gnawing though, praise be to God, so far it had only tucked into the missal. The intruder was very small and swollen in the face, with a crafty look and something, perhaps the blindness in one eye, that made it instantly recognizable.

"Stop, brute!" roared Don Xil. "What you're nibbling there is the Sacred Word!"

The mouse in question turned around without showing any surprise, very phlegmatically, and eyed the speaker from top to bottom, with the hint of a sneer, while wolfing down a furl of paper. Something must have jogged its memory because, adopting a sudden air of diligence, it ran its snout along the lines that were remaining and in the light of the moon spelt out, "A-rius rose up, Ne-sto-rius

30

rose up, Lu-ther rose up, Cal-vin rose up and count-less o-o-o . . .
Blow me down!"

"And countless others," Don Xil read out to lend it a hand. "But
they've all disappeared and the Church is still here."

"Amen!" said the other in solemn retort. "Forgive me, Father, but
I thought it was literature."

"Try to profit from what you've been eating," replied Don Xil, some
authority finally restored. "But don't even think about starting on that
other book. You hear me? Don't even think about it! I won't have you
giving in to temptation, I know who you are. Matacáns, the worst
poacher in Nemancos!"

"All that's nothing but rumour, Father. Envy on the part of those
who use a shotgun! I would have none of it. I'm like you, Don Xil. I
always considered the close season sacred!"

"I would rather you did not commit perjury, Matacáns," said the
priest. "The ferret was sticking out of a pocket of your sheepskin
jacket. And the snare out of the other. You frightened away the hares
for good, Matacáns!"

"Don't delude yourself, Father. It was some chaps from Carballo,
who turned up with a whole load of artillery. And also the stress."

"The what?"

"The stress, Father. It's what they said on the television. The hares
went mad, or something like that. The female was not interested in
the male, who wasn't working either, if you know what I mean, Father.
And so there were no more hares in Galicia."

"But there was one, there was one, Matacáns, that would caper
about the fields and sit in the shade of the vines. It was, it was . . .
when was it you died?"

"It was freezing out there! I wish they'd thought to leave my beret
on."

"Yes, but when was it?"

The other was just working it out when suddenly two greenish

31

beacons appeared in the window, which let in the moonlight. This was followed by a wild shadow cast from side to side of the pane of glass. The two nightbirds observed the phenomenon with curiosity, unaware for the moment that it befitted their rodent condition to get the hell out of there.

"Run, Father, I'll be damned, that tiger's a member of the Resistance!"

"Which one is he?" Don Xil asked as he took to his heels, gasping for breath.

"Arturo the brave, of Lousame!"

As he hurried along at the poacher's tail in search of somewhere to hide in the cellar, the minister lamented the whims of the Lord of Fate, because he too would have liked to be a large beast and to command some respect in those parts. Undoubtedly that cat was not good news; he remembered Arturo of Lousame well, he had been a bagpiper and Xil took him for an anarchist, since once, during a feast-day Mass, in the middle of the consecration, while he was holding the chalice aloft, he had played a few notes from Riego's *Hymn*; the priest was not an idiot, he could hear all right. Not only that, he knew the words to that jangle:

> *If the priests and nuns only knew*
> *what a hiding is coming their way . . .*

It was only a prank, but he remembered him for it. When the time came, he refused to confirm his good conduct and Arturo had to take to the hills, because it was Don Xil, during the war, who governed lives; it made him shudder just to think about it: back then all he had to do was put a cross against a heathen to have them wiped off the map and dumped in some ditch like a rag doll.

"Isn't the Civil Guard anywhere to be seen?" asked Don Xil as they paused for breath.

"It's somewhere about, but Sergeant Maneiro is singing to the same tune, he's a wretch like us!"

"God save us! This world's a jungle!"

"If only we had a shotgun, Father!"

"No talk of love, Matacáns!"

8

"I had three husbands," said the lady.

"Really?"

"Yes, it's true."

And she found the expression Rosa adopted unwittingly so funny that when she reached out for her glass of Lágrima wine, to smother the laughter that was coming, she broke out into a cough and had to use a handkerchief to cover her face since her reddened eyes were streaming. As she calmed down, it pleased her to see that Rosa was smiling as well, now that the salt of her tears had mingled with the sweet wine on her lips. And this amused and at the same time conspiratorial look from the tenant helped her to remember, without being afraid that she might burn herself reading in the fire, in the fragile plates still smouldering in the ashes.

"Just like all those famous artists."

"Just like them."

"Liz Taylor had six at least," it occurred to Rosa to say, enjoying as she was this conversation that allowed her to travel in company to a fantasy interwoven with films and art paper where she would usually wander on her own. "She married the same man twice."

"Yes, Richard Burton. Would you . . . would you believe that I met him once, that he was as near to me as you are now?"

"No way! You're joking!"

"It's the honest truth. You can't imagine what eyes he had! He was a Welsh king!"

"I heard he was a drunk."

"Yes," the lady agreed sadly, as if it pained her to reveal the dark side of an idol who had passed away. "A drunken king!"

"And they used to beat each other! I read in a magazine that they loved one another, but that after they had been together for some time, they were like cat and dog, and one time she threw a typewriter at his head."

"There are so many stories! But how important is the life they led? Now the only truth about them is in the films they made."

"I often recall a film with Joselito," Rosa said. "*The Little Nightingale.* I was very small, it was when Néboa still had its own cinema. Joselito was a shepherd. When he disappeared off the screen, I was convinced that he was walking with his flock through the pine forests of Néboa, because there were fields and a wood just behind the cinema. Once my mother got very angry with me and I told her that one day I'd leave home with Joselito. She looked all surprised, as if thinking what strange things this girl's got in her head."

"I haven't been to the cinema for a while. Good films are always sad. And I'm very tearful. I get hurt."

"I don't know what I'd do if my husband decided to beat me," said Rosa suddenly, looking over at the pram where her baby slept, in the conservatory, along which the wisteria wound with the patience of stone. "I brought you some cigarettes!" she then remembered. And she got up and went and felt carefully beneath the blanket.

"Don't you let him beat you," said the lady very seriously.

They exchanged a glance and lit two cigarettes. Soon the plumes of smoke became friends and intertwined in the air.

"As I recall, Marilyn Monroe also married three times," said Rosa.

"In fact, I didn't marry three times," the lady corrected her. "What I meant is that I had three men."

"Three love affairs."

"I don't know. Yes, I suppose so. Three men."

9

"My father used to hate all this. He was very jovial, very good-natured, and it only became noticeable when mother fell terminally ill. For some reason, something that pulled her apart from us two, she wanted to be here then. I'm not sure, I think that decision, mother's fondness for Arán, hurt him deep down very much. He put a brave face on it, but I realized then that he detested Arán, that he felt an aversion to the manor, not just to the people, but to the house as well. He would grumble at the insanity of the stones, at the things that were old, as if he held them responsible for her progressive malady. He suffered a lot because they would treat mother as if she were seriously ill, with long silences that confirmed the worst possible prognosis, with solemn, exaggerated attention that had the semblance of a fatal rite, the preparations for an outcome that he could not accept. His humour, whenever he attempted it, had no place here. Perhaps what annoyed him most was that she had acquiesced to it all. Whenever we said the rosary, which we would mumble in the half-light, she would collapse into an armchair in the corner and merge with the shadows. All you could see was her wringing her hands. Above mother's bed was a crucifix that seemed enormous to me, placed in such a way that, however you positioned yourself, you could always see the wounds. Whenever you entered the room, your eyes were drawn towards it. If you sat with your back to it, it reappeared in the mirror on top of the chest of drawers. Sometimes I would help mother to comb her hair in front of that mirror and, as I was doing so, I would be unable to avert my gaze from that Christ on the wall who, to my mind, was struggling to staunch the flow of blood, and I found it upsetting that my elders should behave as if nothing were wrong, as if it were the most natural thing to have someone permanently martyred up there with open wounds, nails in his hands and feet and blood dripping from his crown of thorns. Since then, I haven't even been able to look at a crucifix. They give me the creeps. In time, a Lady of Sorrows appeared in her room, on the bedside table, and a vase of lilies. You grew accustomed to seeing mother, her voice sinking to a whisper, pale, wasting away between the white sheets, just another figure on the altar of that room that looked more and more like a chapel. Whenever he went in, my father would lose all his energy. He travelled to Coruña to run the shipping company, but it reached the point where his arrivals in Arán resembled those of a stranger. He felt useless, marginalized and under scrutiny. He began to be obsessed that there was no fresh air in the house, and so he would open a window. But in no time at all someone had shut it. It was one of the aunts, who in turn were obsessed by the draughts, but, instead of confronting them, he would behave as if the windows in Arán shut of their own accord, seemingly convinced that everything, from the cutlery to the hinges of the doors, had conspired with the people in the house and was hostile towards him. Now I think it may have been because he was afraid of them. He and my uncle, who had recently returned from the seminary and was a newly ordained priest, would exchange no more than a grunt in place of a greeting. Uncle Xil was thickset and impetuous, he would shoot down the corridors like a streak of lightning and thunder when he spoke. I couldn't understand how he could take such long strides dressed in a cassock. On one occasion, I was sent to Mass, but I had already been in the morning, and I complained to my father. He sat in an armchair, hidden behind the pages of a newspaper. Without looking up, he said, 'You must do as you're told'. In Coruña, he would sometimes tell me, 'Don't mention this in Arán, don't say anything about that in Arán.' Rummaging through things in the house, I once came across a portrait of my grandfather wearing an unusual outfit with a small collar and embroidered apron. He was standing very upright and straight-faced beneath a caption that said: *The Respectable Light Lodge of Finisterre.* I found this very funny, it struck me as comical, but father snatched it nervously out of my hands. 'Not a word about this in Arán.' They were fifty miles apart, but they were two opposed worlds. In the house in Coruña, any news, the announcement of a boat, of a visit, of a letter, of a delivery, was received with curiosity and joy. In Arán, the door was opened warily. The outsider was met with distrust. Father was an outsider too. Once, on his return, he found that mother had got out of bed. It was a beautiful September afternoon, with the sun shining pleasantly. She had wanted to come out and meet him, dressed as if for a party, with her hair neatly combed. They went for a walk between the plane trees, mother calmly, letting herself be carried along, and father elated, gesticulating and talking the whole time. They paused hand in hand at the Scallop Fountain. I had never seen them like this. I had never stopped to think that they could exist and love one another quite apart from me. I suddenly realized that they could be there and smile and love each other even though I was not watching, even though I did not exist. I remember that I held back and that the scene filled me with sadness, but a different sadness to any I had experienced before. That they could be happy without me was a way of thinking that I could be happy without them. What I felt in front of the tortured Christ was an infantile, external fear, brought on by the horror of an image of extreme cruelty which was on show in the sick-room, and which undoubtedly for me hastened the end rather than pushing it further away. But this agreeable sight of my parents gazing lovingly into each other's eyes while they listened to the murmur of the water really brought home to me the pain of death. I saw it in my mother's smile when they returned and she was nearer to me. She was going and this was her way of saying goodbye. Whoever leaves deposits their sadness on the one who stays behind, waving with a handkerchief in their hand. Whoever leaves is always a little higher: in the saddle of a horse, in the window of a train, on the steps of a plane, on the bridge of a boat. She had the unmistakable appearance of someone who was leaving. That night, father joined us in our prayers and for the first time the whisper of the rosary became for me words that I could hear and understand. They felt to me like stitches, like embroidery needles piercing the skin. Father drove me away from here as soon as he could, he took me almost without saying goodbye, as if escaping a curse, as if he feared that someone might activate a trap concealed in the stones, which would swallow me up. I remember the Ford 28 rattling feverishly along the paving stones beneath the chiaroscuro of the plane trees. The last person I saw was your mother, leaning motionless against the gate, her hair tied up in a Portuguese scarf and her hands in the pockets of her apron. She was young like me, but that day I thought she was a grown woman and I was a girl who was still playing with her dolls, years had gone by for her that had yet to go by for me. I knelt on the back seat, with my chin resting on my arms, and watched her growing smaller. Whoever leaves always deposits their sadness on the one who stays behind. I had enjoyed helping her with her chores. The things she did every day were for me great adventures. It felt like a miracle to hold the rope for leading the cows and that such big animals should respond to the nervous tugs I gave it. One day, they sat me on the hurdle and I had the sensation that I was gliding over an earthen sea, on the waves of the furrows. During the threshing season, we lugged sheaves about and the ears of corn made my blackened, sweaty skin itch so much I scratched like a dog. Climbing over a fence, I cut myself on the brambles and had to lick the blood. Then we went and bathed in the river, a vegetal river that was green, thick with weeds that sprouted white flowers on the surface. It was just the two of us, in league, naked, laughing and splashing one another, protected by the trees. Once, in your mother's house, I asked for the lavatory and everyone laughed, and off we both went to do it in the cowshed, hidden away, with our skirts lifted up over the manure. In the mill, with my eyes shut, I learned to distinguish the different types of flour by the touch of my fingertips. Wheat flour is like silk; rye flour, like wool; maize flour, like linen. If you put your hands in the box full of ground corn, you'll no longer want to take them out again. The mill was a magical place. We could spend an eternity hypnotized by the movement of the hopper and the millstone, while the gurgle of the water reached us through the holes in the ground. And whenever I was out and about with your mother, I heard language, harsh blasphemies and sweet-sounding ballads, that I'd never heard before, as if the tall wall of the manor house had been built deliberately to prevent the words of the village floating in. Memory is a mysterious lady. We do not choose our memories. They live their own life. They come and go. Sometimes they disappear for good. Other memories stick to us like lichen to a stone. They're bits of life that never faded, that feed on the cold air, and increase slowly on the bark of time. I have forgotten many things that I considered to be very important, but those moments as the peasant girl that I was not have never left me: the happy escapades into the world of the servants, the itching of the straw, the cuts from the brambles, the stink of the manure, the green water, the words that existed behind the manor-house wall. I didn't realize it, but it would be those details that would link me to Arán for good. Those details and death, which we were rapidly escaping from, as the car rattled over the paving stones.

'And now I should say, "I don't know why I'm telling you all this." And you, girl, pulling aside the shadows with your fingers, will reply, "You're doing it for me."'

10

Simón walked along, stretching after his early bus ride, and it was there, at Real da Mariña Gate, where the city opens up in a mother-of-pearl shell towards the east, that he saw the seven ladies.

As in the temple at Arán, they were richly dressed, in satins and tulles, velvets and silks, organdie and laces, an apparition of divine carmine, turquoises, blues, emeralds, salmon-pinks, wine-reds, scarlets, tobaccos, lilacs and blood, a jovial and flowery posy heading down from the Old City through the Aires Gate, with an escort of scruffy, hung-over little men, their shirts out and bow ties twisted, but not the girls, they were charming, décolletées at dawn, whispering with laughter, calling out to the sun. What surprised him most was that they were barefoot, carrying their patent leather shoes gracefully in the hand that did not hold a rose, placing such delicate feet freely on the rough, damp early-morning pavements: queens' feet, fisherwomen's feet. Taken up as he was with the vision, the city down by the dock redolent of sex and sea, Simón followed the festive cortège along the colonnade and then down Agar Alley until one of them, when they had gone past the Rosalía de Castro Theatre, turned around to pick up her rose that had fallen, and on standing up eyed him shamelessly. At which point he, to hide his embarrassment, stopped to view the posters outside the Paris Cinema, which was showing a film with Clint Eastwood on horseback, carrying a smoking gun. And when he looked around, the saintly figures were already some distance ahead, next to Blanco Photographs, but what he did see outside La Camisería Inglesa was a circle of people gathered around a travelling salesman who was beginning to tout his wares. Simón drew near to this new source of interest and saw that he had a fold-up table with a green cloth on which the pedlar, with great pomp, scattered a handful of grains of corn and proceeded to produce out of his suitcase a small device with a red plastic handle and a roller made of something like bristle which he gently slid over the emptied contents of his hand. There were no longer any grains on the green table because the red gadget had scooped them all up. The salesman praised this prodigious piece of engineering to the skies, it was only twenty duros, the sweeper, the invention had brought the whole of Europe to its feet, from the governor of the Bundesbank to the king of pizza, they're all using it, his public fascinated as much by the sales pitch as by the magical effect of the 100 peseta brush. Following on from the grains, he scattered a handful of breadcrumbs on the green table, and the wheel passed over them like a cow's tongue and cleared them all. The crowd dispersed, except for Simón, who remained very attentive, with a look that said that a man like this should be in charge of a nation, but soon new spectators arrived and the pedlar scattered flour on the green cloth, a handful of pure white flour, and everyone focused their attention on the hand raised high which slowly descended, the miraculous gadget phosphorized by the light in their eyes, and proceeded to lick up all the flour in a single motion. Then the hawker replaced the golden grains and, before addressing the world, he glanced at the large lad who neither came nor went, motionless before him, his hands in his pockets, his mouth ajar and his gaze fixed on the corn. And Simón, noticing that the gadget had not come down this time, sensing a strange emptiness around him, raised his eyes from the cloth. The two men stood watching each other in silence, face to face. Finally, the salesman, with greater pomp than ever before, scooped up the grains with artistry.

The visitor from Arán combed the city, carrying out the errands that had brought him there, very proud to feel the presence in his pocket of the manual sweeper with its special effects. On the return journey, with all the adolescent turmoil, youngsters from Arteixo, Laracha, Paiosaco and Carballo, Simón started placing small objects on his thighs and put the marvel to the test, so successfully that the teenagers stopped fooling around and formed a public for him. This was nothing compared to the welcome he received in Arán, where he repeated the operation in the manner he had dreamed of, using grains of corn on the table. Pleased by the way that everyone was amazed, visibly moved, Simón went and held the device out to his sister.

"Is it for me?" asked Rosa, drying her hands on her apron, having done the washing up.

The children fought for it, but Simón did not let go until he saw that she had it in her hands. And then Rosa read aloud the small letters tattooed on the plastic.

Made in China.

"I was told that my father saw from the balcony of the Mariña how a group of soldiers placed the pieces of artillery on Parrote Street. When the soldiers began to bombard the Civilian Government, not far from the house, he listened to classical music. When they went to try and persuade him to look for a safe hiding place, they found him lifeless, slumped in the armchair, the needle scratching the silence between the blasts of the shells. His heart had packed in. He had been saying for some time that something terrible was going to happen. His mood had changed and he only ever read bad omens into things, but everyone attributed his state of mind to mother's death, from which he could not recover. The idea of my going to London was at his insistence to begin with. In the shipping company, he had a lot of dealings with the English and besides, of course, there was Gondar, his brother, who had been working there since his youth. Had mother been alive, such daring would have been unthinkable, whether Gondar existed or not. At that time, a girl from a good family never travelled alone, much less to a place that was still strange and distant. But, though it may seem odd, father's mood improved with the preparations for my departure. You would have thought he was the one who was going to fulfil a dream. He planned my farewell, turning it into a festive occasion, and infected me with his enthusiasm to such an extent that I ceased to be worried. There was no drama even when I boarded the boat. I would be home in a year at the latest. Mine was a journey that had a return, with presents when I set out and when I came back. I remember that the same day, in the harbour, the open area in front of Customs was packed with emigrants on their way to America, camped out by parish with their crude trunks, cardboard suitcases or simple bundles with a few clothes. A long queue waited their turn to confess and receive the blessing of a priest seated next to the door of the administration building, a task he performed with a certain lack of interest, perhaps because of the routine or the stifling heat, because he kept fanning himself with his biretta while the person kneeling unravelled his sins. It was the first time I had seen anything like it. Listening to father, I had become acquainted from an early age with the map of cities across the sea, with such exotic names as Havana, Caracas, Santos, Rio de Janeiro, Montevideo and Buenos Aires. I knew that boats left for these destinations almost daily. I regularly went for walks a stone's throw away, in the Méndez Núñez Gardens, and I had never associated those villagers carting packages with a trip to America, which I pictured in my imagination as an expedition of adventurers. That is why, that day, when I crossed the open area in front of Customs, watched in silence by those country-people, holding on to my father's arm and helped by servants who carried the luggage for us, I had the sensation that I was in a foreign port, full of extras taken from the least funny bits of Chaplin's films that I used to go and see in the Kiosko Alfonso, a cinema very near there. How glad I was now to be different, to have on a pretty dress, to be going in the opposite direction, not to have to queue up alongside those timorous girls in their headscarves and men in berets, the ugly pendulum of a tie hanging down to their knees!

"I had Gondar waiting for me! I'd never seen him, I didn't know him, but I had a kind of talisman of his, a cluster of postcards that he had sent me, not just from England, but from other countries that he had visited, images of Amsterdam, Berlin, Prague, Lucerne, Vienna, Venice . . . To me, Gondar was like a magical being who moved in a cosmorama, against a backdrop of quays, tulips, swans, cathedrals, museums, hotel terraces with white awnings next to glittering blue lakes, cafés with large mirrors and streets brimming with strange and elegant people. Each picture that arrived was like an enchanting invitation. I kept them tied with a ribbon from my hair and whenever I undid them, going through them in solitude, the images grew to life-size and I would walk naturally around these places, so much so that when I visited them for the first time, I had already been there, and my companions would express surprise that I should recognize so many things, ask about the minutest details and not be too bowled over by the large monuments. Besides, I always regarded Gondar's handwriting as a secret call, which I read between the lines. It was on one of these postcards, where he normally addressed me as *Dear niece*, that I first came across the expression *Dear Misia*, which seemed to me aimed at someone who had not existed until then, who had been born in order precisely to see themselves addressed in this way. So, unconsciously, as I undid the bundle of postcards in the cabin of the boat that was taking me to London, I imagined a story that would end up happening, although one may discover then, to one's horror, that sometimes the dream itself becomes possible because someone, somewhere, sets a nightmare in motion. I arrived in London during the first days of July 1936. It really was like stepping into a fairytale. Gondar turned out to be a charming and amusing man and a protective uncle, the ideal companion for that young lady who wanted to be a woman without ceasing to be a girl. He lived in a beautiful brick house with a white wooden porch in a smart district, that of Mayfair, which in those bright summer days resembled an enchanted rose garden. For me, it would always be the house with the copper beech, a tall tree that stood out at a distance with its broad crown of red-tinted gold. Soon after I arrived, when I was still in a state of shock, unsure of myself, like a butterfly that has just emerged from its chrysalis, I found out that a war had broken out in Spain and that my father had died of a broken heart. For many years, I did not want to hear anything about what I had left behind. Sometimes, sometimes all I could see was that vision, like a fixed photograph, of the queue of emigrant children waiting for confession with the shapeless, rhomboidal ties hanging from their necks. Aren't I boring you with all this?"

"No, not at all, madam. I like the way you embroider the story."

12

And there was a solitary Barbanzan pony with white hoofs living in the gullies of the Penas Cantoras, the jet-black skin prettily painted with snowflakes, biting with its green lips at the balsamic broom flowers and the dainty soft gorse, pondering sadly on the book of inner colours, because it was in its own way a survivor.

The Barbanzan's mother had died in the snowfall at sea of 1964. This had coated the estuaries and high crags in white, bringing lapwings and wolves to the seashore. There are days when the sea-gulls miaow like cats and this was one of them. It remembered that it was freezing, stuttering childlike whinnies, caught between the fright of its dead mother and the wonder of seeing snow on the sea's boundary. Most of the green-moustached horses from the Barbanza mountain range had also died in the snow, but in a distant exile, on the Russian steppes, frozen on remote paths or with their guts savagely sliced out of them – there were soldiers in the Great War who would sell their soul for a draught of horse's blood to revive the stiff bell of their throat, or to warm their hands for a minute at least in the hollow of the entrails, to nestle there their inert bodies, at the glacial limit of existence.

And to flee another chapter of memories, the old lamp of the moon lighting its mother's wake, the Barbanzan pony hurriedly bit a thorn in amongst the shoots that made it paw the ground and pronounce a curse.

"Jesus Christ!" said the crow, who had come to land on the topmost crag, which was enamelled with lichen.

The Barbanzan looked askance at the hooded bird, attempting to conceal its interest, because it was better, it thought, not to encourage these rapscallions.

On receiving no reply, not even a measly thank you, Toimil gave the password that awakens the memory of the buried kingdom. "*Vivat Floreat Natio Galaica!*"

Albar, the horse, then intoned an amen which came straight from the heart. The hooded bird could not be an outlaw talking like that. Besides, as a beast of the country, he was not servile but he was sociable.

"I have come from the king of Galicia," said Toimil. "He has ordered you to go down to Arán and allow yourself to be captured."

"To be captured?" asked Albar in surprise. He did not wish to appear insubordinate, but the idea hurt him as much as the thorn in his gum. "And hasn't His Majesty heard of a beautiful invention they call freedom?"

"Of course he has! It is his coat of arms, his lineage!"

"And so?"

"But this is a special mission . . ."

"I have not been branded," the Barbanzan observed with melancholic pride. And, as he said this, he felt the horror of the hot iron stamp, the stink of skin charred with slavery, the outrage of the uncouth scissors brutally pruning the long mane, the savage whoop from human throats during the taming of the wild horses, the drunken cock digging his starred spurs into the horse's kidneys. "I don't want anything to do with people, I'd rather wolves."

"This is a favour His Majesty asks of you."

"And who's going to ride me?"

"An innocent."

The Barbanzan was standing in a field, by the cultivated limits of

Arán, picking out clover and mint to calm the anxiety in his stomach, when he saw a man approach in a blue riding jacket and Mexican sombrero, a sickle under one arm and carrying a huge radio cassette player under the other, which was blaring out music. *Every step I take, I find memories of my mooooother.*

There was no doubting who this was. The crow squawked in a clear sign from the chimney.

Horse and man regarded one another. The king of crickets chirped out of the music box. *For the orphan there's no sun, because everyone wants to be his faaaaather.* This – Albar – is Simón, an angel hewn with an axe in the workshop of hell. He's about your age, he also remembers the snowfall at sea of 1964, the burning fingers in the snow. This – man – is the old white horse that comes from the paradise of eternal youth, from the great orchard where hours are counted in pippins. It was Simón, then, who took a step forwards, having set down the cassette player and sickle, and he did so very slowly, as if the field were a carpet of glass, not wanting a violent outburst to chase away the dream, the vision that he grasped tightly, watching devoutly, holding on to the air with his arms outstretched and his palms facing downwards.

A few of the farmers walking along the edges of the fields, others who peeped over hedges and walls, were witnesses of this other miracle: Simón, the mute from Arán, was conversing with a horse. In a low voice to start with, in affectionate murmurs and loving fisherman's cadences or spelling out caresses with the powerful odour of mountain talk. The disbelievers could see the words in the air, concentric rings suspended in the valley's atmosphere. And those voices, the first used by humans, sounded good to Albar, who only moved as a game and to delay possession a little. Whenever Simón came closer, the horse responded with a gesture of indomitable irony, either by snorting, by pinning back his ears, or by nibbling at the ground, but he kept his hands, both front and back, still. There was a moment, a few yards away from the beast, when the man understood that he was the one on trial: it was when he saw his reflection in the pure jet of the animal's eyes. No need now to rear up and crack open his head. He had powerful hoofs, crowned white, a pretend mallet in each hand. From wall to wall, the pagans of Arán were laying down bets, and expressions of dread, with their eyes. Simón did not take long to think about it, the horse had a noble air, and with sweet nothings he shortened the remaining distance, he was an arm's length from the mouth, and knelt down and picked out mint and clover and held out the handful as an offering to the old horse's lips. The Barbanzan took a delicate nibble and savoured the present. The man rose cautiously to his feet and with the hand that had made the offering gradually approached Albar, finally stroking the skin with his fingertips, whispering in his ear, "Here, boy, here," until the mute finally embraced him, necks entwined, offering kisses, "My precious, my love."

13

"All of Gondar's friends were women, and this made him more attractive. As in a romantic novel, I could say that I was already in love with him then, without realizing it. But it was something that could never have crossed my mind, that would have gone against the nature of things, an impossible sentiment. My way of looking at it was: I love my uncle, my father's brother, very much. In the company of those ladies he took great care to behave like a gentleman, like a character from another time, adopting a manner that was both confident and warm in his treatment of others, flattering the petty vanities of whoever was in front of him, always putting himself forward as the target of his own irony. His profession of shipping agent he defined as that of a refined corsair. As a Spaniard, he was loyal to a republic that no longer existed. He remained a Catholic, because it allowed him to feel truly incredulous. 'The day you stop laughing at yourself,' he used to say, 'is the day others will start laughing at you.' Most of that curious circle were women who shared his disposition, cheerful and timeless, figures that had emerged from a painting and were waiting to go back in. It was some of those friends who kept me company when the war with Germany started and Gondar began to get busier, not showing up at the house with the copper beech for days, sometimes weeks on end. What amazed me was that, whenever he was absent, there was always, always one of those ladies ringing at the door with 'a pretty plan' for me, although the city had been turned upside down by the bombs. Such is the way of things, I never felt as protected, as close to a people, to a country, as when the air-raid sirens sounded in London.

"The nightmare of the war was followed by days during which it was forbidden to talk about suffering, when everyone endeavoured to make up for lost time, to feel alive and to celebrate it. It was during these festivities, at a well-known fancy-dress party which took place at the Albert Hall, that I met Kadi Nabar. I went as a Moorish princess on my uncle's arm and he introduced me in a way that gave the impression I had recently arrived from a land of fantasy: 'This is my niece, Misia of Arán, who comes from the ancient kingdom of Galicia.' He happened to disappear for a moment and someone put a glass of champagne in my hand that was really very cold, and I could feel the tips of my fingers freezing up and then, would you believe it, the cold ran like a current through my entire body, affecting my voice as well, so much so that I couldn't speak, an attack of nerves, and all I could do was smile, a fixed smile, like this, as if my skin had grown rigid. My legs wouldn't work, if I wanted to take a step with the right, the other went forwards, it's not funny, I came over all dizzy, with people talking to me and the light of the lamps dancing in my eyes. After that, everything turned very unpleasant. I felt ridiculous and lonely standing there in the middle. What is more, for the first time in ages, I felt foreign, as if the dress had aroused a dormant anxiety. The truth is I was almost crying when I reached the end of the hall and sat down on a chair. I closed my eyes and I don't know how much time passed because I was no longer aware of the commotion or of the inconvenience of being in fancy dress. What I could hear, and don't laugh, was a stream, a murmur in a place that, to start with, was unknown to me, water pushing through royal ferns and then cascading down a rock surface covered in moss and navelwort, and you can't imagine how relieved I was to run my hand and eyes over the moss. Lost, I returned to a corner of Arán. But I had to open my eyes and get out of there because someone was asking me if I felt all right. I saw him leaning over me. He was a very dark young man, with incredibly thick eyebrows, at least that is what caught my attention because he was very close, as close as you and I are now. I smiled at him, without revealing anything more than a smile, but immediately I noticed that my skin had softened and my fingers had warmed the wretched glass. So, as if to gain time, I took a small sip and felt in my lips that I could speak now. 'I'm here with my father' – what a nutty thing to say, but those were the first words that came into my head. And so he answered me, 'Well, that's great, I'm here with my mother.' He burst out laughing. I was very embarrassed, but then he asked if he could sit down next to me. When I looked at him properly, despite the severity afforded by his eyebrows, I found that his features were almost child-like. He was a strapping boy, a teenager placed in a suit prematurely. 'I've just been around the world,' he told me. Then he said, 'I have a fear of lifts. During an earthquake, it is better not to be in a lift.' 'That's right, earthquakes!' I replied with amusement. 'Every day there's an earthquake.' 'No,' he said. 'Not every day. But I have one that's pursuing me.'

"And it was true.

"Kadi Nabar was Armenian. He had been born in a village of the Bosphorus and that day the earth had trembled. His family interpreted it as a sign and left for Baghdad. After another tremor, they moved to Cairo. Kadi encountered that earthquake in other parts of the world. He learned to see it coming. He discovered that there was always a dog somewhere that emitted a howl of warning, a kind of unmistakable lament that put him on his guard. 'So,' said to me suddenly, 'if you'd like to share an earthquake, you can marry me.' One night, in Bombay, when I had already forgotten about that joke, he woke me up and asked me, quite naturally, whether I could not hear this lament, which was the dog of the earthquakes warning him. First of all, I turned over, unsure whether I had entered or come out of a dream, because it was true, I could hear a dog and it hardly seemed possible that the premonition of a solitary animal could fill the night so completely. But there was a point when I came to suddenly and my heart leaped so that I appeared sitting up on the bed, gazing wide-eyed all around me, in a state of panic, you can imagine, knowing that something terrible is about to happen in the world and the person who is in on the secret is telling you that it is better not to move, that it would be madness to go wandering about the hotel corridors in a nightdress at this time of the night, and pulls you gently towards the pillow, holds you in his arms and says, 'Don't worry, my love.' It wasn't long before we noticed that the whole building was swaying very slowly, not with abrupt movements, but being rocked like a cradle, while all we could do was to watch in silence as the plaster petals crumbled from the ceiling rose.

"That was my first husband. Kadi was rich, immensely rich. 'That admirer of yours,' Gondar had said to me good-humouredly after our first encounter at the Albert Hall, 'is swimming in gold. In black gold.' His family owned vast oilfields in Iraq. Needless to say, after that," the lady said to Rosa with a conspiratorial smile, "he struck me as even more agreeable and interesting. But he really was both these things – rich and agreeable. After we were married, our only occupation was to avoid getting bored. He taught me an Italian proverb: 'Money does not bring happiness, but it calms the nerves.' I remember once, in a hotel in New York, we were given an extremely large bill because our Pekinese had wet a carpet. Kadi very calmly went and asked the price of the carpet. It was a huge carpet that virtually covered the floor of the lobby. The manager then appeared, very nervously, to offer an apology, but Kadi interrupted him, 'Be so kind as to have it wrapped, I shall take it with me to Europe.' We spent a wonderful period in Paris, in a house right in the centre, on the Avenue d'Iéna, which had pheasants in the garden that would sometimes jump from the terrace and stop the traffic. We were like two children, in love, rich and happy. We occupied the time travelling, laughing, playing games, attempting to surprise one another day after day, waltzing! Our separation came about overnight, as if while dancing we had left a hall and there was no garden with pheasants, but an enormous void.

"I could not get pregnant, nor were we overly concerned, we were in no hurry, but one day, one day, a doctor who had treated me for an infection went and told us that it was very likely, that he had the impression, that he was almost almost sure, that I could not have children. It hurt me to discover this, but to tell the truth, at that precise moment, I didn't mind too much, in reality I was even more of a child than he was, and I waltzed, waltzed at all hours. Kadi said nothing, and smiled in encouragement, taking hold of my hand. But a few days later, when we were with his family, the matter cropped up in the middle of the conversation, and I could see quite clearly that this news had cut the air. His mother's face hardened suddenly. In the bottom of her eyes, I observed with rage something that had never affected me before: contempt. I glanced at Kadi and saw that he was white as a sheet, that he was frozen inside, and mouthing like a fish out of water. All his good humour, all his childlike determination before earthquakes, had come to naught. This surrender I had witnessed on his part awakened the spirit of revolt inside me, and suddenly it was as if Kadi were a stranger, one of those faceless shadows you spot walking along in the rain, an intruder in my life, someone who had taken me by the hand through a rose garden and deserted me right on the edge of a cliff. That's how I felt there, goaded by half a dozen pairs of eyes that demanded of me something like an explanation of the inexplicable, that I apologize, that I make amends in some way for this anomaly in my nature. I was a young lady, a *señorita* from Coruña, brought up to believe that I was beautiful, elegant and happy. Also discreet when I had to be. I was not ready to endure a blow of this calibre so soon and I longed to go to my room and cry. But then this fury erupted, as unfamiliar to me as it was beneficial, a fit of anger that prepared me for everything that followed and that I carried out resolutely. I put down my cup of tea, stood up with a smile and explained that it had been a pleasure meeting them. I went to collect my gloves, handbag and coat, for it was cold and drizzly in London, just as it is here now. They were taken aback, silent, and then a rising murmur followed me down the hallway. He came after me. 'What's up, baby? Don't be like this, Misia, you've got it all wrong. Wait, wait.' But when I turned around, by the front door, and looked him in the face, I knew that there was no way out, that I could not ease my purpose, that something fateful, a worm of bitterness, had entered our lives, because he knew it too, although he was asking me with reddened eyes not to go.

"We never saw each other after that. Not even with lawyers as intermediaries. But he behaved very correctly, very properly. For a time, he tried to send me money, but he no longer insisted when he discovered that it was all returned to him. I know that there were occasions when he helped me in secret, influenced his friends if he thought I needed it, and sometimes I noticed that it was his hidden hand gently opening the door. He remarried, at least twice, I think, but nor did he have children by those women. He once wrote me a letter from Portugal. 'Dear Misia,' it said, 'do not forgive me. Please never forgive me.' Then he wrote, 'With nostalgia, I await an earthquake in Lisbon.' I learned that he had died there, in a hotel room, but not of an earthquake. He had gone for a few days and, without anyone knowing quite why, he just kept on prolonging his stay.

"No, love, it's nothing, I always cry a bit at this part . . .

"After that, well, I wasn't interested in men that much. Suddenly, memory appeared to couch me in despondency. I saw myself in Arán, embroidering in the sun lounge, sitting in a wicker chair. Or one day I would amuse myself walking the streets of my Coruña in the form of odours. Sweets from La Gran Antilla, cod fillets from La Tacita de Oro, spices from Bernardino Sánchez, Siboney coffee, chocolates from La Fe Coruñesa. These I could mix with others that rose like a damp mist towards the manor house: the carts of manure pulled by steaming oxen, the colony of gulfweed in the mouth of the river, the gorse that livened up the hearth when the days were short. But I also knew that it was forbidden me to go back at that time, that behind the good memories and the innocent landscape lay dozens of tongues in wait, sharp as Taramundi knives, the terrible vice of human sacrifice. I was too young to let them flay the skin off me.

"It was Gondar once more who gave me the strength to continue. Gondar and the house with the copper beech. He took me in again and made me recover my strength and a little happiness, enough to want more, in the knowledge that all the love that comes free when you're young is taken away after the first painful disillusionment and, at that moment, you must become your own guardian, you must keep track of your own sentiments and store up all the happiness that you reap, all the better to digest the outside world, as a spider uses its juices. So there I was serenely picking up the pieces, keeping myself very much to myself, finally confident that I was a grown woman, when the type of man I could least have imagined walked through the door.

"Joker was the opposite of a dream. A bloodsucking journalist, who made his living precisely from couples falling out of love. He wrote gossip columns on the rich and famous. He was always the first to announce disagreements, reveal infidelities, inform of imminent divorces. He reported on meetings and weddings as well, but without the same success. 'Happiness,' he used to say, 'is an ephemeral news item. Newspapers would die of happiness. Bad news is lots of news.' He wrote a section entitled 'The King of Hearts', but he was really better known under the nickname of *The Gravedigger*. His fame preceded him as an author of obituary notices. In these, he only had good things to say about people. Many hated him, and quietly despised him, but they were very careful around him, however much he might have martyred them with his stories. He was convinced that his great power came from the obituaries. It amused him greatly to have control over the Last Judgement.

"That was my second husband. He had come to see me because he was writing a book about oil magnates, and more specifically on the Nabar family. I told him straight off that he was not going to get any information out of me, that I did not intend to spill the beans. To my surprise, he did not insist. Then he called to tell me that he had abandoned the idea of that book: 'I shall write one on you instead, the beautiful woman who left the oil king!' This frightened me senseless, but it was only a joke. After that, I began to see his horrible loud ties wherever I went, and to hear his wicked clown's thunderous laughter. We became friends. Sometimes I would look at him and ask myself what I was doing there, next to this miniature devil who mocked happiness and every day flew over the city like a vulture in search of unfortunate victims. But the question ceased to make sense as soon as he entered the stage grinning mischievously from ear to ear. Life was a comedy, a spectacle, why not go along with it, why insist on taking it seriously?

"Joker was a cynic, set in his ways, a liar and, sometimes, a real outlaw. His manner, his form of going through life, pretending, taking advantage of people, and people being aware of it deep down, but playing along and even flattering him, seeking his presence rather than fleeing it, this fascinated me. It was a side to the world I had no idea about. There were many things I was ignorant of. Things that had to do with human nature. For example . . . for example, I believed in sins. I believed in sins just as I had when I was a girl. I knew that I could commit a sin, but I was also sure that I would realize, that I would say, 'Well, I have committed a sin and what's done is done, or this requires a penance'. I could not envisage another way of looking at things. What attracted me in Joker was this immoral approach to the world, this shameless way of being selfish, this courageous lack of scruples. Everything enveloped in a silk glove. There came a point when I found myself saying of certain situations, 'This suits me, or this doesn't'. I think I had come to the conclusion that with this type of man I could be free and at the same time protected. And I was right. Because he then went all the way with me in the role of besotted knight, as if he had drawn a circle around my name and decided to make of it an island. He asked for nothing in return. For him, I was something exotic, I represented a kind of weakness. I could see only slaves around me. In high society, and in low society as well. With him, I was not a slave. To anything. To any obligation or any feeling. And in fact it was living with him, thanks to living with him, that I really began to love Gondar. My uncle loathed Joker, he behaved as if the other did not exist. But deep down, he also knew that, had that devil not entered my life, I would never have had the strength, I would never have been able to do what I did."

It was Rosa's heart now that beat vigorously in the silence that followed, while the lady's fingers embroidered melancholies in the Camariñas lace. Vegetal forms. A maze of tenderness on which to rest the eyes.

"Yes, Gondar and I were lovers," said Misia, without waiting to be asked, as in the old days, when cautious siege was laid. "I lived with Joker until he died. I felt great sorrow, I loved him in my own way. And he had not planned to die so soon. I think he was convinced that death would show him a degree of deference. One night when I returned home after visiting him in hospital, I began to sift through his papers. And do you know what I found? I found a file with the obituaries of people who had not died yet. They were ready to be published in the newspaper. All they were missing was the date of the person's demise."

"Good heavens!" exclaimed Rosa. "He'd taken their measurements!"

"One of them was Gondar's. Joker knew things about him that I

60

could not have imagined. What was written there was the biography of a stranger. Is it possible to live with someone who belongs to the confines of a story and not realize it? Gondar turned out to be an actor, an invention. He was married. He had a son. Joker depicted him as an anonymous hero. He had directed a network of spies made up of Spanish republicans in different parts of the world. During the war, he had been decorated in secret by the English. It would seem that, during those absences which I had taken to be business trips, he was involved in hazardous missions. After reading this, I couldn't even be sure he was my uncle. Who knows when and how the story had begun?"

"What did you do?"

"Nothing. Certain things must continue until the end. You have to give life a free rein and let it breathe a little. You have no right to go asking someone for an explanation with their obituary notice in your hand. We were happy. When he did die, no newspaper remembered him. I made an effort then to trace his wife and son, but no-one was able to tell me whether they truly existed. In reality, no-one could tell me anything. At the burial, I was alone, in the rain, watching the water run into the muddy grave that held the coffin."

"And had he written you an obituary?"

"No. Joker never wrote anything about me. Not even a line. Not even a romantic poem. It must have been true that he loved me."

"Not a word about this, you hear me, Matacáns?" Don Xil said from the hiding place, in a severe tone of voice that betrayed his inner turmoil. "These are family matters!"

"And who would I preach to, Father?" the other replied, still confused by the story that had been related. "Here, there are no more than mice!"

Night was falling down the gullies, between the Penas Cantoras. Enchanted by the story, Rosa had forgotten the time and was sorry to have to return to the world. The child had not stirred in the whole afternoon. "This baby," she said, "really is the devil. His sleep's all up-ended. I could put him under the tap at the fountain and he still wouldn't move!"

When she opened the front door, she discovered the flock of sheep, impatient to enter the manor house. She waited with the pram until they had gone inside and watched as they huddled together in the main hall, next to the staircase of honour, where Misia's shadow fell across the marble. Then she cried out to herself, as she was swallowed up by the darkness,

"My husband! He's going to kill me!"

14

Back in the cellar, Matacáns gave the priest some newspaper pages to try that were piled up in a corner.

"Sink your teeth into this, Don Xil, it has a more cured taste."

The paper was stained yellow like lard. El *Ideal Gallego*. Franco, a dozen trout in the River Eo, one grouse in the Ancares, a lot of holes at the Golf Club, five death sentences at the house in Meirás. Franco's wife, Doña Carmen Polo, and her friends from Coruña went to see *Gone with the Wind* yesterday, at the Equitativa Cinema.

"This is what's known as feeding off nostalgia," said the priest ironically, while gnawing at the headlines.

Matacáns: "What?"

"Nothing."

"And now to combat heartburn," said the poacher, winking his good eye, "what would you say to a muscatel?"

Don Xil noticed that his heart was thumping like a sewing machine. His pinprick eyes glinted in the dark. "What's that you say, Matacáns?"

"What you heard, Father. The stuff in the bottles is pure vinegar and the casks are as empty as bass drums, but there's a small barrel, Don Xil, that's blood of Christ."

"God bless you, Matacáns! Let's go and sample the miracle."

On turning around and following the way the other indicated, the priest felt a strange presence, a flitting shadow that alerted him and detracted from his enjoyment of the moment.

"There's someone else here, Matacáns!" said the priest, pulling nervously at his tail.

"Someone? What do you mean, someone? This place is full of people, Father. Reliable people. You just have to watch out for the little people, they're small and quite fierce, I don't know where on earth they come from. They must be bandits!"

The poacher climbed up some pegs and skilfully hauled himself up on to the top of the small barrel. He swore an oath under his breath. The lid had been recently nibbled and a few dead lay floating in the wine.

"Is anything the matter?" asked Don Xil impatiently from below.

"Everything in order!" said Matacáns. And he hung down to the spigot. "Now, Father, give that bowl a good tilt, we don't want to lose any of this vintage." As soon as he was satisfied with the arrangement, he very cleverly opened the tap, which at first produced only a trickle, but which then became a flow that poured out like a rose into the bowl.

"God bless you, wretch!" Don Xil murmured with emotion when the drops splashed his snout. But just as he was about to drink from the bowl, taking care not to upturn it, he heard a babble of voices, which became more and more familiar as they approached, voices that criss-crossed and overlapped in a chaotic festival of the memory. But he had no time to look around because he found himself surrounded by a boisterous rabble which, drawn by the sweet jet, had emerged from beneath the stones, most of them mice, but there were also toads, spiders, fleas, ants, cockroaches, bees, snails, slugs, moths and even a bat that manoeuvred recklessly from the beams in the ceiling.

The Spider: "This thread of silk, just as you see it, in the same proportion is stronger than steel."

The Toad: "The flies I like most are the ones that have been on the ham."

The Cockroach: "They're like very sensitive little hairs which tell you which direction the blow's coming from."

The Ant: "To tell the truth, it hasn't changed our lives much. We breed a kind of louse, tame as a cow. The milk is condensed milk."

The Flea: "I feel like Superman, but in miniature. With these elastic bags, we can jump the equivalent of 650 feet. I wish we'd had them before!"

The Bee: "I can't see so well, but there are advantages. For example, in the antennae are incorporated some chemoreceptors which are very useful for picking up smells at a distance."

The Snail: "Pardon my French, what pisses me off is the rheumatism. Rheumatism when alive, rheumatism when you're dead too. Might it be an ailment of the soul?"

The Bat (passing by): "At 100,000 hertz!"

"That's Gaspar," Matacáns explained, once more at Don Xil's side. "Do you remember? The one who had a put-putting motorbike."

"By the nails of Christ!" exclaimed the priest. "Half the parish is here!"

"What are you surprised about? With the recommendation we had, they didn't want us in Heaven, or in Hell for that matter," said Miranda not unreproachfully, the spider who had been a seamstress.

"It's no use crying over spilt milk! Let's drink to the health of everybody!" Matacáns toasted, in an attempt to parry the blow. "Gaspar, could you *please* quieten down?"

However, everyone stopped still, in amazement, their senses on full alert, because in a crack of the wall, emerging with some difficulty, a lizard had appeared, of monstrous proportions in their eyes. When it reached one of the shafts of light pouring in through the chinks in the ceiling, the stranger's back gleamed the different colours of the rainbow.

"Forgive the intrusion," said the lizard sleepily. "I'm still a little dopey from the winter, would you be so kind as to tell me where I am?"

"These lands are at the end of the earth," informed Donalbai, a snail who had been a quarryman.

"Then I'm not so far out of my way."

"And where were you hoping to get to, if you don't mind the question?"

"To San Andrés de Teixido!"

Everyone crossed themselves at the mention of the sanctuary and chanted in unison: IF YOU DON'T GO WHEN ALIVE, YOU MUST GO WHEN YOU HAVE DIED.

"Allow me to introduce myself," said the lizard, encouraged by the quorum of voices and by the providential tickling of the beam of light. "My name is Marcial Requián, producer of crimes, at your service."

The identity of the stranger left the parishioners perplexed and once more distrustful. The silence ended up being somewhat embarrassing, and the saurian felt obliged to expand a little.

"I mean, I was a producer of crimes for film and television. I had to invent ways of killing and dying."

"Plenty of work in that," observed Borborás, a toad who had been a musician in the Caracola Orchestra of Néboa.

"Work was not lacking, no," said the lizard with a certain amount of nostalgia. "As you know, any film worth its weight requires plenty of stiffs – pardon the expression – and what's more, people don't like repeats. Even if a thousand die in a war film, you've got to give it some imagination and vary things a bit, so with one his chest bursts open, with another his arm drops off, another spills his guts, or spits an eye out through his mouth . . . The easiest ones were westerns, but then things got complicated. The ones I found most boring had modern weapons, in which the dead are simply blown away, and that's it. Lots of computer. If there's no body, if there's no blood, then the art has been lost."

"Is it true that the blood is in fact tomato juice?" asked Miranda.

"No! There are lots of ways."

"Tell me," Don Xil joined in, having remained very attentive, "how many people have you killed yourself?"

"Well now, that would be hard to say. Things got much busier with television. There were days I had to elaborate deaths even in my lunch break. One that got a lot of publicity was of a man who bled to death after plucking a hair from his nostril. Everything I did during the day turned into a possible scenario for getting rid of people. I would go to a party with some friends and while they were talking about a pleasure cruise down the River Nile, I was imagining which would be the most spectacular way of placing a corpse in that house, whether cut up inside the fridge or distributed in tiny pieces, in the form of croquettes, on the trays of snacks."

"That's enough to drive anyone mad!"

"Uh-huh," murmured the lizard. "I didn't realize what a tunnel I was in until I tried to get out and it was too late. The situation grew distressing when I began work on a TV series about suicides. It was called *Farewell, Cruel World*. As a specialist, I had to suggest original ideas for taking an early exit to the scriptwriter. Everything was going more or less OK until another channel started up a similar programme called *I'm Leaving*. It turned into a dogfight for the audience. 'Take it further, take it further!' the directors spurred us on. Classical methods were no longer valid. No hanging yourself in a barn, no gas, no throwing yourself into the sea. Present company excepted, that's the sort of thing a child would come up with. You had to shock people! One episode met with a lot of success, in which the protagonist, out of spite towards a love that had left him, decided to kidnap his ex-girlfriend. He tied her to a chair and, before her very eyes, prepared his suicide. He stood on a large block of ice, turned on a heater, tightened a slip-knot around his neck and . . . He didn't die until the ice had melted."

The liquid hammer of the tap sounded the knell in the bell-shaped bowl. The deceased parish watched in horror as a man on the imaginary screen lost his footing while time subsided in a pool on the ground.

"That's outrageous!" said Don Xil, unable to hold himself back any longer. "It goes against the Law of God."

"You are right, of course," said the lizard pensively. "But we beat the record of audience. Without wishing to offend, I don't think God takes much notice of TV series."

"How about you?" asked Borborás, to satisfy everybody's curiosity. "I mean, how did you . . . ? You understand."

"The rate was unbearable. I had to take tranquillizers. I didn't exactly want to die. I just wanted to rest, rest properly, get a really long night's sleep. One day, after work, I realized I'd lost my head. That is to say, I was having thoughts I didn't want to have and I could no longer control the thread. Suddenly, I got very frightened. I looked at myself in the mirror and I said, 'Marcial, you've got to sleep.' First, I took a couple of pills, then another couple . . . I still haven't woken up."

15

The chore Rosa enjoyed most was combing her daughter's hair, Anabel was her name. She had given her this name on account of a TV soap that had made her cry a lot. This other Anabel was in love with her father, but she did not know that he was her father, good-looking as he was, even though he had gone grey at the sides, a real gentleman, but Anabel thought he was just an old friend of the family who had come back loaded from Miami to . . . Where was it all this took place? Whatever, Anabel's father, the one who was but wasn't, was in love with her as well, so Anabel loved her father and her father, the mother's husband, loved her too. For her part, the mother, Anabel's mother, was still in love with the father, Anabel's real father, i.e. her ex-husband. Now that she thought about it as she combed the child's hair, it sounded like a joke, but back then, pregnant as she was with the girl who would later be Anabel, my word, she had cried her eyes out, sitting on the sofa of the three-piece suite they had just bought, that smell of new furniture covered in imitation leather that reminded her of days, days of . . .

"Quieten down, you!" In particular on Sundays like today, in the morning, when the reborn sun hard on the heels of winter warmed the front of the house, and she sat the child outside in a chair and combed her hair, combed her long locks, leaving them like silk, gold threads in my hands, fair Anabel, my princess, don't grow, don't be a woman, stay like this for ever with the toy dog in your arms. But today, today she had to take a good look at the hair at the back of her neck and behind her ears because, well, because the girl keeps saying it itches and won't stop scratching, what on earth could be wrong with her, she's always so clean, not like before, my goodness, what misery, the stables inside the house, only the water from the well, and taking a bath – taking a bath! – taking a bath twice a month, and let's not get on to the subject of food, it's obvious in their hair that they eat a lot better, look how it shines. We should thank our lucky stars . . .

"Quieten down, girl!" I can't believe there's anything wrong with her, what could be wrong with her, but I suppose I'll have to look. Who knows what she comes across at school!

And then she shouted, she became so hysterical, she shouted, "You little bastard, you shit!"

"Let me see, Mummy!"

"Shut up, you!"

". . ."

"Stop crying! Well, I'll be damned. Look, look." She held it on the pad of her finger, it still moved.

"It's got six legs!

"The cheap little bastard! The pig!"

She had forgotten quite what they looked like and this one struck her as enormous. Stunted, hard, with its sucking head, parasite of the warm blood of my daughter, look at it kicking, you can even see its pincers. Is it a female, do you think? I wonder how they do it. It must have covered her head in eggs, nits stuck to her hair, I'll look at them one by one, my child, if I have to, we've all Sunday ahead to rid the lice from the locks of my princess.

And she went to the kitchen and came back with a plate of vinegar. Better like this, one by one, with my hands, I'll have to get some of that stuff from the chemist's, how revolting to have to go and ask for it, I'll use my hands instead. Her head crawling, how could I not have seen them? The pigs sucking at my baby's neck, sticking their pincers into her gold threads.

"Who do you play with at school?"

"There's one who's always got snot hanging out of his nose."

"Do you play with him? Does he stand next to you?"

"No."

"Then don't lay the blame on him."

"I play with Patri, Luci, Milagritos . . ."

"Oh, forget it. Who knows where they came from."

Later on that night, when her husband returned home – he now worked and had business to attend to on Sundays as well – she told him that the girl had lice. She was in bed, awake, her eyes wide open in the dark. He was lying next to her, with a dead left arm on top of the mattress.

"I've got wind. You know? I think I might be pregnant . . ."

He opened his eyes then, but didn't say a word.

16

Simón had no time to rest, attending to the livestock and the vegetables and giving Rosa a hand with the kids, especially the baby who was still being breast-fed and crawling about. But Cholo, his brother-in-law, thought he was lazy and stupid as well and he couldn't stand that Mexican music that always went about with him, be it in the fields with water up to his ankles or cleaning out the cowshed in amongst the steaming cows and gorse manure. There was something else Cholo hated about Simón: his eternal smile, the happy calm of his countenance. And not just that: the love between brother and sister, the mutual protection between wife and mute.

He found him a job and told him with a pat on the back, "You're going to be a man, Simón."

"Thirty years old! What's a bloke doing at home at thirty! Wiping kids' bums? He'll earn a salary. He'll be a man."

"But I'm all alone," Rosa had said.

"Look at him out there, he's happy. He's even conversing with the horse."

Simón rose at the crack of dawn and attended to the animals. Fresh grass in the cowshed, maize and greens for the pig and in the hen-house. For Albar, a royal mix of oats, barley and bran. Last of all, he took his bread and milk, seated on a stool in front of the Barbanzan. Before going, thinking of Rosa, he lit the fire on the hearth. He put on the blue Prussian riding jacket with pocket flaps and red edgings, positioned the walkman, arranged the mariachi hat, and off he went, on horseback, over the hills, escorted by the king of Galicia's army, in the direction of the Néboa sawmill.

Albar trotted along happily. He could hear the frozen pine needles crunching under foot. He felt at home in the deep cart-tracks, old vegetal galleries with arches of laurel and holly. A blackbird's "good morning". Not even the sound of an engine in the distance. The horse was surprised to hear a man singing, who turned out to be his own and seemed as a result lighter and to be singing in time to the trot. *I want to be shot down riding my jet-black pooooony.*

"The truth is," explained Toimil to the king of Galicia, "I couldn't tell you for sure whether it was a sad or a happy song. That Mexican music gets my senses all confused. The point is that Simón and Albar arrived at the sawmill a few minutes early. A group of operators were warming their hands around a stove made out of an oil drum using sawdust as fuel. When they caught sight of him, they burst out laughing quite unashamedly."

"Mary Mother of God!" said one who was from the area of Santa Comba, "Who's the general?"

"Simón dismounted," narrated Toimil, "and went towards them with his cordial smile, not worrying about taking off his hat and headphones. They responded to his greeting, but didn't stop cracking jokes, all of which our boy took to indicate a friendly reception. The foreman, on the other hand, was fuming when he arrived shortly afterwards."

"Hey, Ricardo! Have you seen the artist Cholo's sent us?"

"It's Jorge Negrete! Ha, ha, ha."

"Oy, you!" the steward shouted at Simón, gesturing energetically. "Take the headphones off!" he said, pointing to his ears. "Get rid of those dummies!" And he pretended to take the headphones and throw them on the ground. Then he added, still gesturing to the purpose, "Those clothes, get rid of those clothes! Wear like these! See? You've got to wear clothes like these to work! What you're wearing's fine for the circus. Circus! Understand? This is not circus!

"For the circus," he repeated softly. It was then that he noticed Albar for the first time. "Blow me down with a feather! And that horse? Where did that horse come from?"

"He brought him, boss. The Lone Ranger!"

"You came all the way from Arán on a horse?" the one they called Ricardo asked Simón, imitating a trot, ta-ca-ta, ta-ca-ta, with his voice and fingers. "Holy Mary! Who's this I've been sent! At least you've a strong back!"

"How did his day go?" asked the king of Galicia.

"He did the work of three or four," said Toimil. "He felt good lifting pilasters of wood in the air as if they were towers. And he likes the smell of sawdust and shavings. Me too. What happened was that at the end of the day, the other workers hid his mariachi hat and his walkman. They're not a bad lot, it's just the custom on the first day. But the poor lad couldn't understand what was going on, the reason for such unkindness. He sat down on a log and burst into tears. And then one of the others, the one from Santa Comba in fact, upset at seeing that giant with reddened eyes, gave him back his treasures."

"Don't bother bringing that contraption tomorrow!" the boss said, pointing to the walkman and shaking his head. "The machine can take your fingers off, understand? Rraaaas! And there go your fingers!"

Simón looked silently at Albar. They were standing two feet away.

"And if you want to come on horseback," the boss said finally, "that's up to you." He approached Albar and stroked his neck.

"That's a pretty horse. That sure is a pretty horse!"

17

Everyone in Arán was an assiduous reader of El *Caso*, a weekly news-paper that published accident and crime reports, but only once did the parish have the honour of appearing on the front page. It was on the occasion of the murder and passion of Gaspar the bat. They were keen for Marcial Requián, producer of crimes for film and television, to hear the story from the mouth of an exceptional witness of that memorable event.

"Get down from there, Gaspar!" Don Xil shouted now imperiously.

The bat drew a striking ellipse in the air and then came to land on the spigot of one of the empty casks.

"Look here, Gaspar. This gentleman," explained the musician Borborás, pointing in the direction of the lizard, "is an accredited authority in the world of accident and crime and in the art of crimi-nal entertainment. Albeit modestly, on account of your case, we had the privilege of seeing our village appear in print in the history of crimes of passion. Tell him what happened."

"I prefer to forget," said the bat sadly.

"Make an effort, Gaspar, as if you were telling a story!"

"Someone give him a drink," Matacáns advised.

"Come on, Gaspar!" the parish encouraged him.

"You have my most respectful attention," said the lizard. "Having staged them myself, you've no idea how much I envy a romantic death!"

"All right then. I had a sweetheart in Germany. A girl who had come from Turkey. She was slim, petite and dark-skinned. I would pick her up and it was like taking hold of a flame. She had these black eyes that set fire to you, but at the same time made whoever was looking feel light as a feather. I don't know if I'm explaining myself very well."

"You're doing fine!" said Borborás impatiently.

"She loved me, I hadn't appreciated how much, as you'll see, even more than I loved her. The thing is there was a third, another man who was after her and who came from her country, from the same village, they were neighbours almost. All three of us worked in the same factory and that complicated matters, you can imagine, what with the exchanged glances, looks of longing from us but from him looks that cut like knives. He thought that she belonged to him and he came to tell me this one day. I, I don't know, I ended up accepting it, resigning myself, not out of cowardice, God no, but out of habit, because we're made this way, in tribes, I don't know, I got used to the idea that she was meant for him. The truth is I stayed away from her, I didn't look at her at work, I didn't answer her messages, I didn't turn up at our rendezvous. One day she came up to me, in the factory, and asked me what was going on and I, I . . ."

"Don't stop now, Gaspar!"

"I told her to leave me alone, it was over, the end, *Ende, machen Schluss*, understand? not to call me, see you around, girl. And she went and right there stuck a knife into my chest and I fell, I fell slowly, gazing at her lovingly, without it hurting, because the knife went straight into my heart and stole away the pain I had of days and days of bitterness. It would seem she then killed the other. More than twenty stab wounds."

Judging by the pause and the expression on the faces of the parish, everyone was watching the cellar's screen, as the slim, electric arm vented its anger on the intruder twenty times.

"That's where things went wrong," explained Don Xil to the lizard, "they got the bodies mixed up. They sent the other's corpse to Arán. It arrived in a zinc coffin, which had been carefully sealed. The Germans are a conscientious lot. But people wanted to see Gaspar's face in order to carry out the wake properly. So we opened the coffin with some blacksmith's scissors. And there was the other."

"So what did you do?" asked the lizard, impressed.

"What do you think? We sent it back. And they did the same. Besides, Gaspar only had one stab wound."

"And what happened to the woman?" asked the lizard.

"The woman? How should I know!" exclaimed Gaspar melancholically. "She used to sing songs, the kind the sea plays on the radio at night."

18

"I don't want to have this child," said Rosa without crying. "I can't have this child."

It was the eve of St John's Day. The bonfires had burned, towering luminaries. Their laurel crowns had burst into sparks that faded now, scattered over the valley floor like homesick fireflies. She had gone to see Misia after dinner, when the children were asleep and Cholo and his brothers prolonged the evening playing cards, moored in thick delight to montecristos and cognac, following on from the feast of sardines and spare-ribs, happy to be in each other's company, at ease, with no women or children.

"I'm going to take these herbs to Misia," she had said, in her hand the bunch of everlasting, fern, elder, reed-mace, laurel, camomile and fennel, the seven essences of St John to wash the face with and guard against curses.

"And the wine?" he muttered without taking his eyes off the game.

"That as well. I'm taking her that as well."

"I win. Hearts," he said, striking the table with his knuckles as he threw down the card. "Don't be late. The baby might wake up."

"I don't want to have this child," she said to Misia. "I can't have it."

She realized that she was not crying, that the words flowed of their own accord, fell neutrally through parted lips, she was aware of the stab of pain in her stomach, knuckles that probe into entrails, a random card.

"There was a time I really loved him."

She was crying now. How good it was to feel that hand so different to her own, a caress of bones delicately held together by the old skin. A hand, however, that was incredibly strong, warm, noble, friendly.

"It's true that we really loved one another. I remember, I remember when he had emigrated to Switzerland, shortly after we married, sometimes, sometimes I would sit in that old car he had as a young man, in that old Fiat left in the barn, I would take a radio and put on some music and imagine that he was sitting next to me. I would light a cigarette, like this, and then say thank you as I blew out the smoke slowly, like this, towards his eyes, the way I'd seen in films. Can you imagine, how ridiculous!"

The two of them were smoking now. Thank you, Lord, for the silver bridge that carries us over from tears to laughter. She took another sip.

"It might be raining outside and I would imagine it was the two of us driving along a glistening road and he would take a hand off the steering wheel and stroke me between the legs. This really turned me on. You won't believe it, but on my own, in the barn, stuck in that old car surrounded by farming utensils and trusses of hay, full of spiders, with music and smoke, while I watched it rain outside, I would get really, really randy.

"Yes, I loved him a lot. I would cross off the days on the calendar. I don't know what went wrong. I really don't. I look back and I honestly couldn't tell you when it all fell apart, when we went from using tender words to spiteful ones, when we started moving away from each other in the bed or doing it like machines. I don't know. He's like a stranger to me, one of those blokes who look you up and down if you're alone. When we're doing it, when he's on top of me, I think it's someone without a face. He could die and I wouldn't miss him. God forgive me."

79

19

Don Xil felt the evening bell in his heart. He was in the attic, trying to digest a page of classified advertisements that the wind had left in the vicinity of the manor house and that had attracted his attention, because in amongst the flats and second-hand cars for sale, he had come across some unexpected offers, such as: *Extremely young house-wife, punishment, total humiliation, extremely beautiful, sensual. Generous breasts, perfect feet. Call me, you'll be my slave automatically. Video. Hotel. Home. Visa.* Or others that were much more direct, for example: *Sandra. Kinky.* This was followed by a telephone number. Now, those women's names joined to a number to arouse desire, albeit mercenary, had been melancholically nibbled away by the mouse of time, the old hunter-priest who peeps out through a chink in the attic and contemplates the lights in the valley of Arán.

"What's this about *elite*, Father?" asked Matacáns, who was still trying to read, opening wide his good eye, taken aback by the section's novelties, and making use of the sentimental carbide of the full moon.

"*Elite* is the best, the pick of society," Don Xil responded without taking his eyes off the nativity scene and unaware what the other was driving at.

"Elite," Matacáns read. "*Top Notch, Superendowed, Gorgeous, £120. Also Visa.* And this about Visa, Father, what's Visa, for goodness sake?"

"Cut it out, Matacáns, that's quite enough!"

"Thirty thousand pesetas to have it off!" the poacher continued.

"Whatever next!" And he raced down the stairs, muttering about former prices in Coruña's Papagaio Street. But he soon showed his face again in great excitement and roused the minister from his reverie.

"Don Xil, Don Xil! There's an infidel downstairs!"

"Stop pestering me, Matacáns. Leave me alone."

"One of those Moors who sell carpets, Father!" the half-blind mouse announced happily. And he ran back the way he had come.

Don Xil followed him lazily at first, weighed down by thoughts of what was and what wasn't, but then, on drawing near to the cellar, he quickened his pace and arrived in time to hear that dusky mouse in fine Frenchified tones telling the story, as if it had happened to someone else, of how he had been run over and killed on the road leading to Arán. The strangest aspect of the story was that it had only just happened, right there, that very evening. Mohamed was walking along the side of the road, covered by his stock of carpets, when a car zoomed past, veering into the ditch and knocking the poor man down from behind.

"They drive like lunatics!"

"They're a curse!"

"What hurt me most," said Mohamed to the assembled parish, "is that they didn't stop. Before my last breath, I still had time to hear them accelerate away."

"Shameless!"

"Animals!"

"The same thing happened to a grandfather of mine who was run over in Coruña," Borborás recounted. "He always used to say, 'I've not been killed in two wars and a car will get me.' And that's how it was."

"And the carpets?" Miranda asked.

"There they remained, stained with blood," said Mohamed sorrowfully. "They were my final resting-place. I had some very attractive ones as well, with pyramids and diamonds, like the Shiraz carpets of Persia, and other lighter ones, pretty like the Kars from Turkey, or the Hamadam, which are Iranian."

"We only had one, by the bed," said Miranda. "I can still feel it next to my feet at dawn, the sweetness of getting up in the morning. We bought it after the wedding, in El Palacio de las Alfombras, on San Andrés Street. You know that shop opposite Nova York in Coruña?"

"When I was in Coruña," said the quarryman Donalbai, "I only ever stopped to visit the recruiting office when I was young and the surgery when I got old, over in Orzán. What I do remember, though, is the Borrazas bar. I used to have a brandy coffee there after seeing the doctor."

"You went to the Borrazas?" exclaimed Mohamed gleefully. "They let me set down my carpets there and I would drink my tea."

"There were at least twenty cages with canaries and goldfinches," Donalbai recalled. "After the surgery, they were like spring. Then they installed a television and one day they got rid of the songbirds. They told me it was because people complained when there was football."

"And do you . . ." Don Xil said suddenly, addressing Mohamed, ". . . do you believe in God?"

"Naturally," said Mohamed.

Cholo's business started going well. He was working on his own now. He succeeded in buying a plot of land which he then resold for a good price and he soon became proficient in these transactions, so much so that he found himself with money he had never had before. He was already thinking of going into partnership with his brothers: it was a good time to be building and selling. There was another circumstance that promised to change his life. Bernardo, a neighbour from Arán, from a family who were nicknamed "the Mugginses", was elected councillor in Néboa. The two families had never got on particularly well or badly and initially the election had not bothered Cholo either way. He had no fixed idea about politics: in any case, it was a word he used contemptuously. That was how he had always heard it pronounced. Franco had restored order, he had tightened the reins on an ungovernable country. This was also what he had always heard. One day, in Switzerland, a fellow worker, a Galician as he was, by the name of Iglesias, had talked to him of fighting for an amnesty for the prisoners in Spain.

"Amnesty? What the hell is amnesty?"

"Freedom," said the other.

"Freedom? They can go and stick it, they shouldn't have got into trouble in the first place! I'm here to work, understand? To work. Do they put food on the table?"

The other had looked at him in silence. He was not expecting such an angry response.

"He can go and stick it as well, a bum-sucker like me," Cholo had muttered, digging the spade into the pile of sand, when his workmate walked away.

Muggins' election had given him an excuse to make fun of the newly formed democracy. "If he's a councillor, then so could I be, ha, ha, ha." In fact, neither of them had voted. Rosa had not even thought to, and he had used the holiday to act as an intermediary. But months after that, Cholo started referring to Bernardo without using his nickname and in the tone of someone who is talking about a friend. One day, they arranged to have lunch at a steak house on the Néboa road; another, they travelled to Coruña together. And even though he hardly ever said a word to her, Rosa was pleased at all this. His business, his relationship with the councillor, the new position that was on the horizon, gave her hope that their personal life would also improve. She was expecting another child, when the smallest was still not walking. She felt tired. It was an effort to smile in front of the mirror.

One morning, when she was tidying up the bedroom, Rosa opened the drawer of the wardrobe where Cholo kept his papers. There were the title deeds and, in a corner, next to the marriage certificate and the social security card, the bank-books. She carefully removed the two with red covers that belonged to the elder children, Anabel and José Luis, opened with the money given to them at their first communion, as if they were gold plates. Then she looked at the marriage savings book, the one that had blue covers, and went through the figures, quite a lot now, if only Mum could see it! She was about to put everything away when she decided to open the box file that Cholo had used ever since he was in Switzerland. There were things, payrolls and the like, that she did not understand, but there were also some of her letters sent from Arán. One of them with her lips printed in carmine and a farewell: *All yours.* She sighed and inserted the letter back in the pile of papers. It was then that she saw another, purple savings book, with the logo of a bank that was not theirs. She took the book out of its plastic holder and opened it in the middle. The figures danced in front of her eyes. She went to look at the beginning, running her fingers over the pages. Whose could it be? Perhaps a mislaid document that Cholo had found somewhere.

Simón.

Something strange, a shriek of fear, galloped through her chest.

Simón Paz Oliveira.

She could not believe her eyes.

The bank-book had a sheet of paper stapled to it, which she read incredulously. It authorized transactions on that account on the part of Simón, the account holder, signed with a cross, in favour of José Manuel Carballo and Bernardo Suárez.

That night, Cholo found the bank-book next to his dinner plate. He said nothing. He put it in his back trouser pocket without standing up. Rosa was furious, it was obvious from the washing up, a frenetic clattering of dirty dishes in the sink.

"Will you please be quiet?" he shouted without turning around.

"How can you be such a bastard?" she said as if talking to herself, spitting out the words amid the nervous chink of the dishes. She did not want him to see her crying.

"That money's ours! Don't you see, you oaf? Ours! Or did you think I wasn't going to tell you?"

Water whirling around.

"I was going to tell you, otherwise don't you think I would have kept it in a safe place? What do you imagine, I was going to keep the money?"

Water washing away the dirt.

"What's it to him, he's an innocent. He'd do anything for us. It's better that he never knows."

Water running down the drain.

"You'll see, my love, you'll see. We'll leave this damned misery behind us. It's not like we're stealing. Everyone's at it, anyone would

85

do it if they could. I'll buy you anything you like. How about a ring? You always said you wanted one with little stones. How about it, girl?"

Water dying.

"We'll move away from here. We'll live like kings."

21

"God, to me," said the lizard, "is an interesting word. Who do you think invented it? Was it a carpenter who banged his finger with a hammer, or a farmer grateful for the rain after a long drought? Was it first a prayer or an oath?"

The lizard said this deliberately, hoping to provoke a reaction from the priest, but the latter remained deep in thought, looking nowhere in particular, as if he were indeed searching for a word with wings in the air.

"God, China, Orange . . . How do words come about? Who was it that first called the sea *sea*? That word arose out of surprise, I'm sure of it. There are words that came about because of fear, and others that bear the mark of sympathy. But a word like *sea* arose out of surprise, a three-letter immensity. It's the same in French, *mer*, and in German, *See*. Were the sea to be called, for example, *sealant*, *seamster* or *seasoning*, it wouldn't be nearly so big. And that's why *second* and *minute* are longer than *hour*, which has one more letter than *day*. What was the first human being's feeling when they addressed God as *God*? Was it a king at the top of a tall tower or an old man steering a mule? Were they happy or sad? Were they confident or fearful? Did God want to be addressed as *God*? Was he the one who whispered his name in man's ear? An interesting word, yes sirree. There have been countless wars and deaths in the name of the merciful God."

The lizard said the last bit to see if Don Xil would finally be piqued and join in the conversation. But the priest, rather than disputing the point, agreed, the green beacons of the cat stuck in his memory.

"I signed some of those sentences."

"I can't believe that," said the lizard, taken aback by this.

"I did, my friend. I blessed the war between brothers, I railed against the persecuted, I stoked the fire as much as I could."

"What does it matter now?" Matacáns intervened, having ceased to nibble at a sports page on noticing an unusual despondency in the priest's speech. "It's water under the bridge!"

"At least you repent," said the lizard.

"Repent?" replied Don Xil. "That's fine for children!"

The minister's voice sounded hoarse, bronchitic. Apart from him, not a soul could be heard.

"There's only one way to resolve it, and I know what it is. By paying the whole price."

"Please ignore what was said at the start," Marcial Requián requested, alarmed by the dramatic turn taken in the conversation. "They're just the tangles of a frustrated poet. In between crimes, I always enjoyed poetry. It was my portion of religion. There are prayers that are beautiful poems and true poems, poems made with strips of skin, are no more than devotion, human orisons."

"There I agree with you," said Mohamed, the carpet seller. "Many poems have I prayed on the way."

"Are you a poet?" the lizard asked in pleasant surprise. "Do you write?"

"I talk to myself as I go along."

"Why don't you recite us a poem?"

"They're things that are related to the journey. I forget them."

"Oh, come on, just give us one piece!" insisted the whole parish.

"All right then, here goes:

> For Urika, for Urika,
> for Urika, where my heart is,
> for Urika, for Urika,
> there's no other place quite like it."

"Beautiful," said the lizard.

"I just made it up."

"Urika. Is that the name of your village?"

"That's right. The vale of the seven waterfalls!" said the Berber, closing his eyes nostalgically.

"Waterfalls?" Matacáns frowned. "I always thought that was all desert."

22

And they left Simón in charge of arranging the planks that came out of the sawmill, since they saw that he enjoyed the task of erecting the pilasters, which was important and laborious, and had to be done well, since they have to be as light as they are solid, built like a tower, with the planks in a perfect square, arranged in pairs so that the air can circulate as in a granary and the planks can sweat a little and dry. He applied himself from morning to night, only resting to have lunch, and if no wood had been cut, he would pile up the scrub and the bark of the pines in the form of a haystack or make mountains of sawdust in a natural line like a chain, and the other operators only made jokes so that he would stop for a minute, but deep down they were proud of that hardworking mute who was transforming the chaotic landscape of the factory. When they realized, the towers formed in measured symmetry a castle-like enclosure, in which there was a fenced-off area where Albar might roam loose, unaffected by the machines and the heavy lorries. In each of the four corners rose a tower with coloured cloths in place of flags, and on the minaret of a turret that stood out in the centre he placed a sprig of laurel, a detail that was much appreciated by the workforce of the sawmill, since it is believed to protect against inclemency and evil. The mute's benign presence was clearly noticeable in everything, even in their speech, since everyone began to talk more calmly and profoundly.

"It's bloody easy to mind one's language! It'd be easier if it weren't for this fucking weather!"

"I tell you, it's blasphemy that pisses me off. God damn it!"

"Look at our mute. Always happy. He's just a big baby."

"And why shouldn't he be? We were all robbed of our childhood."

"Come on, it wasn't that bad!"

"When I was little, my parents gave me a rod of myrtle the first day I went to school. 'What's it for?' I asked. 'For the teacher,' they told me. 'So that he can beat you.'"

"It's all down to ignorance. And misery."

"Don't talk to me about the bad times!"

"People are how you make them."

"People are how they want to be."

"You're quite right."

"You're not wrong either."

"And what happened with the teacher? Did he beat you a lot?"

"I went the first day and after that I never went back. We were a big family, and I was sent to my grandparents' house to graze the cows. Those were the days of black bread! I still don't know how to read. Well, I can read music."

"Music?"

"Yes, an uncle of mine knew music. He played in an orchestra in Néboa, the Caracola. During the war, he came back to his parents' home with something strange in the head. They said he was a bit mad, but I never noticed anything. He treated Don Hilarión Eslava's *Music Theory* like a sacred book. On Sunday mornings, while the others were at Mass, we'd sit outside on logs and he'd use a stick to draw five lines on the ground, like this, what they call a stave. Then he'd teach me the notes and how to mark time with my hand."

The operator took a piece of kindling-wood and drew a small score in the earth. The other looked at it as if it were a magic script.

"You can read that scrawl?"

"It's the only thing I can read," said the operator.

He hummed the beginning of a song. He moved his hand, black from the resin, like a baton. *If only one day I could reach up to the staaaaars.*

23

"I'm leaving," said the lizard on the morning of St Peter's Day.

The sun shone radiantly. The world stretched. Hearts beat rapidly. The spiral of the weather coated matt skin with enamel. Gypsy souls darted from the quiver of chrysalises.

"If you pass through Betanzos," said Don Xil heavily, "be sure to visit St Mary's Church. It's quite something. There, resting on bears and wild boars, is the tomb of the only feudal lord to be called 'the good'. His war cry was: 'Make bread, baking ladies!' "

"I will. I like stones," said the lizard.

"And don't forget the Betanzos Balloon, a hot-air balloon with drawings and caricatures from the year. It's released at midnight to the applause of onlookers!" Matacáns chipped in.

"When's that?"

"On 16th August. And if you stay for a while, don't miss the new wine. It's served in cellars with laurel at the door."

"I'll drink to your good health!"

They watched him go in sorrow. Before the sun mounted the skylight, the lizard still had time to turn around and take his leave: "Don Xil, Mohamed, pray for me, each in your own way. You've no idea how much I envy people their faith!"

"I liked that sinner," said the poacher when he lost sight of him.

"We should have gone with him, Matacáns!"

"Don't torment yourself, Father." Then he added with an impish smile, "Better days are ahead!"

The poacher, who never wasted his time, had been on the trail of a hoopoe and had finally discovered where its nest was.

"How many eggs do you think there'll be?" the priest asked Matacáns.

"Well, I don't know, but enough to make a good omelette."

With the poacher in front and Don Xil straggling behind, they climbed the tallest wall of the ruined part of Arán manor. But it was not easy to reach the nest, not even for two scurrying souls like themselves. The wall was like a thick vertical forest, covered in ivy, brambles, honeysuckle. Even gorse grew where it levelled out on the top. It was more difficult to find a way through the vegetation and avoid the thorns, long and sharp like dozens of daggers, than it had been to clamber up the stones.

"I can't take any more, Matacáns!"

"Don't stop now, Don Xil, we're almost there!"

"I feel dizzy."

"Shhhhh!

"Now," said Matacáns, stopping at an elevated location that served as a belvedere, "now we have to wait for the female to leave. She almost always does so from here. But we'll have to tread both carefully and quickly, you understand, because the male keeps watch from the branches and she's back in a moment."

It was not long before, from the thick vegetation at the crumbling corner of the manor house, Don Xil saw the hoopoe take wing, black-spotted crest atop the helmet of this fierce, colourful bird. Now was the time. Don Xil ran after the poacher as best he could, tearing through the gaps which the latter opened boisterously. Until he saw that he had finally come to a stop in front of the nest – crudely protected and smeared with excrement – and, without further ado, had leaped inside.

"Matacáns, Matacáns!" Don Xil hissed from outside, only with difficulty preventing himself from retching. "This absolutely stinks!"

"Do as I do," whispered the poacher from inside, "hold your nose and eat. There's a couple each!"

Don Xil steeled himself as never before and finally jumped into the dung basket. Matacáns had already polished off one of the eggs and was poking his snout into the second. The eggs were ash-grey, pretty and shiny.

"They're just right," said the poacher, licking his lips. "They haven't hatched yet. Come on, Father, don't hang around. If the mother comes back, she'll have our guts for garters!"

Satisfied as in the olden days, but enveloped in a nauseous stench, the two friends looked around in the field for a patch of good grass on which to rest in perfumed bouquet.

"Pig!" shouted Matacáns. "What does she have to do that for? Why does she fill her children's cradle with shit?"

"Because of us mice," said the priest.

"She's right," Matacáns understood. "There's no animal that would get this dirty for a pair of eggs."

"We would. In that, we're human," Don Xil philosophized.

24

Leaning on the counter of O' Satélite, the men were nostalgically reading the future in the rose-like dregs of their wine-bowls. There was
complete silence at this time in the bar of Arán. On the morning television, a tenor was singing opera and the powerful sound seemed to
have intimidated the parish in the bar, who were usually quite
animated. Suddenly, Bento Lobeira, who worked in forestry and who
had his arm in a sling, turned around and gazed defiantly at the screen.

"Shut your face, animal!" he shouted at Pavarotti.

This acted as a sign of liberation. Mato, the bar owner, walked
along the altar refilling the chalices.

"Long live Ribeiro wine, and the barman can shove it up his arse!"

"Amen," said Mato.

And Spiderman, who had worked in construction in New York,
explained that he had never had an accident in the workplace until a
saw sliced off his middle finger.

"What height were you working at?" Bento asked.

"It must have been, it must have been about a thousand feet."

"A thousand what? You must be joking!"

"What do you mean? The Empire State measures 1,250 feet. And
we were pretty near the top. Or do you think I'm making this up? You
look down and it's like seeing into an ant's nest, tiny little dots like
thousands of berets around the cars. There are a lot of people in the
world . . . I sure as hell was up there! It must have been more than a

thousand feet! At that height, it's just the Indians and us Galicians. Some of my workmates were from Carnota and we'd share chorizo up there, over New York."

"Chorizo?"

"Yes, chorizo. It was smuggled in. There was a chap from Muros who was found with a ham and twenty chorizos in his suitcase. Since they wouldn't let him bring them in, he sat down and ate the whole lot, there in Customs."

"A ham and twenty chorizos?"

"A ham and twenty chorizos! He said to the guard, 'Well, I'll be damned if you're going to eat them.' He told it to me like this, 'It almost killed me, but I ate them.' "

"Is it true what you said?" Bento asked. He seemed deeply intrigued by something.

"What was that?"

"That at the top there are only Indians and Galicians."

"At least on the building where I worked, yes. Galicians from the Costa da Morte and Navajo Indians, from a place called Gallup. That's right. Why do you ask?"

"No, nothing," replied Bento pensively.

"Hey, Spiderman," said Mato from behind the counter. "Tell them the one about the chap from Carnota who . . ."

"Ah, yes! Well, there's also the one about the knife grinder from Nogueira de Ramuín who arrived in New York and, up on Fifth Avenue, he bumps into a fellow countryman who asks him in surprise, 'And how did you arrive here, with all the papers that are needed to get in?' 'How did I arrive?' he says. 'Well, it's very simple. I walked in behind a wheel!' Ha, ha. But the story Mato was referring to happened to me, I mean it happened to a friend of mine, who was from Carnota, and it turns out the first thing this man did with his savings was buy himself some dentures, because the truth is his teeth were a mess, rotten, in short, a disaster; his only hope was a new set of teeth. And

96

that's what he got. The man was beaming. 'Look, they're an artist's!' he'd say, opening his mouth wide and pointing to his brand new teeth. But one time, in a bar in Brooklyn, this guy picked a fight with us. He was drunk, noticed a strange accent and started from there. He took it out most of all on Carrizo, the one with the brand new set of teeth, who was as big as an ox. Full of patience, Carrizo just let him get on with it. And then one of us went up to him and said, 'Carrizo, this guy claims he's going to smash your teeth in.' Carrizo went, looked the guy up and down, took his dentures out slowly, formal as you like, and placed them gently on a beer-mat. The other was amazed.

" 'What the huck do you want?' Carrizo then said.

"And, with this, he smacked him so hard the other fell to the ground.

" 'What the huck do you want?' " Spiderman repeated. They were all laughing so much they had tears coming out of their eyes.

Suddenly, the television showed some images of a bitch suckling kittens and the parishioners disappeared once more into the screen.

25

The imp of autumn rolled down the lanes, turned somersaults down the slopes, ran shouting down the deep cart-tracks, waved his arms about in the orchards, banged the gates, whistled at windows, and shook the banners unfurled from the clothes-line in the fields vert of Arán, when Rosa noticed that this last effort of hanging the clothes out on the line, against the wind, had been a rash, excessive struggle. A warm liquid ran down her thighs.

"I saw her put down the tub," Toimil told the king of Galicia, "and then cling to her stomach with a pained expression. The strong wind, a south-easterly, caught up her apron and skirts, and in each gust her hair streamed behind her like that of a wounded Amazon."

Rosa looked anxiously about and saw no other living creature than that devil of a crow permanently on the lookout from the chimney-top. She felt so alone that this time she was grateful for its ugly presence. A hook pulled on her belly from the centre of the earth, the grass entangled her feet like nets, while the wind pushed with brutal force in an attempt to fell her. She would willingly have gone down, her face pressed against the coolness of the ground, had it not been for that unfortunate bird which reminded her of the proximity of the house, the bed with the quilt decorated with birds of paradise embroidered in false gold, the wedding photo and those of the children's first communion on the bedside table, and that other, of her mother, hanging on the wall, an old-fashioned portrait with a halo of brightness on a dark background, meeting the gaze of the imp lurking inside the camera, her hair tied back in a bun, high cheekbones, a pained smile with clenched teeth, hands searching for something solid to hold on to, Mummy, mother in heaven, push, push, the lamp so high, so low, threatening, children only belong to their mothers, if the light would explode, with clenched teeth, shouting out.

"It is true that children only belong to their mothers," said Toimil pensively.

"Was it hard?"

"It was, my lord. I was on the verge of taking off to the heights, I was so overcome. A chimney, as you well know, is like a funnel that swallows the sound of the world, but it can also be a horn blasting pain.

"The idea of giving birth at home," Toimil continued, "was because she did not want to move from the bed. She'd reached the bedroom slowly, on her knees, and told the children to go for help and they came back with Spiderman and two or three others who were in the bar. They wanted to put her in the car and take her to Coruña, but she said that the baby was coming, there was not time and she'd rather die than be moved from the bed. Spiderman took the car and drove as fast as he could to Néboa to find the doctor.

"When the father came home, at night, the girl had already been given a name."

26

And one day Rosa went to see Misia, surprised that she had not come to visit after the birth, and discovered the other woman. Wrinkled, withdrawn, dressed in mourning. It was as if old age had entered suddenly like the wind through the keyhole of Arán or underneath the door, bringing all the dry leaves. What scared her most of all was the fear encapsulated in the lady's eyes. A crippled beggar hobbled on the trail of verdant nostalgia. Her speech was quiet, kind but distant, as if Rosa's arrival had interrupted a conversation with other guests. Rosa made an attempt to hide the horror of her first impression, she did not want to hurt the lady's feelings, she was well aware of the damage that can be done by others' eyes, as much as by words. For the same reason, she said nothing to begin with that would indicate her surprise at the state the house was in, abandoned to its fate, or in the slightest at her appearance, which was certainly shocking now that she could see her up close, she was all bones, grey-haired and, why not think it, had surely not washed in a long time. Only after showing her the baby girl, kitten wrapped in the fur of the blanket, and discussing the birth – firmly resolved that never again – only after all this, did she ask, "How are you, Misia?"

"Before I forget, Rosa," she said in reply, "I've something for you."

On watching her stand up and slowly climb the stairs, slippers with holes in, socks over woollen tights, checked apron on black skirt, she thought she had become a typical old lady, one of those grandmothers who shell peas in the porch of time. It was obvious, when she returned, that she had combed her hair and put a bit of colour in her cheeks, and also that, upstairs, she had made a collection of energy and smiles.

"These are for you. I don't want to hear a 'yes' or a 'no', because it's all decided."

It was a small nickel silver chest.

"But, madam!"

"They're for you."

And, without paying any further attention, she carefully pulled the blanket aside to uncover the baby and rub her wicker fingers between her fingertips.

"Let me hold her in my arms for a moment. You'll have given her a name from the movies. Or not?"

"Hmm. I've given her my own name."

"Rosa, Rosiña, Rosa. May there always be a rose in Arán!"

"But, Misia!" Rosa exclaimed on seeing inside the box. "They're your jewels! There's no way, madam. I can't take these!"

"If you don't take them," Misia said in a very serious voice, "I'll throw them into the sea."

"But . . ."

"I'm not lying to you. If you don't want them, I'll chuck them over a cliff and that's that. I don't want some twit from my family making off with them. I don't want them adorning faces I do not know. They're for you. They belong to you."

She started rocking the baby, *eeeea, eeea, ea, a*, as she walked slowly around the hall with a happy expression. Rosa saw the beggar in Misia's eyes move back for a moment and heal his wounds, seated on the marble staircase, his crutches laid out on the steps. She also saw two mice racing towards the kitchen, hugging the skirting boards. All this confused her. The box of jewels in her hand, Misia dressed as a grandmother from the village with the baby girl in her arms, autumn's dry leaves rolling across the carpets, the mice showing themselves in broad daylight; outside, the song of the wind, that persistent howling, savage and sad, descending from the throat of the Penas Cantoras.

"Madam," she said suddenly, trying to appear calm, "why don't you go to Coruña? The cold weather's approaching. You'd be so much better off in your flat in Coruña!"

"Coruña? Ah, Coruña!"

She went back to rocking the child, her smile wounded. She was going to say, Everything I loved is now dead. But no, when had Misia ever complained? She turned around, laughing once more.

"Do you know what happened to me last time I was there, in the Mariña flat? Some friends came to see me, poor dears, all of them more gaga than I am. I invited them round for tea and cakes. Well, after we'd been chatting for a while, I suddenly got up in a tizzy and told them that it was very late and I had to go home. Without giving them time to reply, I gave them each a kiss and left, saying that I wouldn't bother them any longer."

Rosa listened with fascination. "Then what happened?"

"I realized on the stairs, as soon as I touched the wood of the banisters. I said to myself, 'But where do you think you're going? Are you completely off your head?' And I went back. They all thought it was just another of Misia's eccentric jokes. But no. The truth is I can't get used to the city any more. It's my fault. I want to be alone, look after the sheep, feel my feet sinking into the mud, listen to the wind and the rain, notice how the bed slowly warms up next to my old body. The preoccupations of a *señorita*!"

"I'll come and clean then."

"Don't even think about it!"

"If you need any errands run, I'll send the kids."

"No, not the kids," she said with a sad smile that once again belonged to the beggar in her eyes.

As Rosa was leaving, afraid to look around, exorcizing a bad feeling that hung around her, she heard Misia call out to her, as if she had something important to say.

"Hey, Rosa! Rosa!"

"Yes, madam."

"You look very pretty today! You look very pretty!"

That night, for the first time since she could remember – when she got up she would just comb it in a hurry, tie it in a ponytail – that night Rosa combed her hair with a tenderness she had always reserved for her daughter's, she calmly removed all the knots, oblivious to everything around her, to the children fighting, to the sound of the TV, to her husband's arrival, until her hair fell over her shoulders in long, shiny waves. Slowly, she tried on Misia's jewels, noticing some traditional silver pendant earrings and then the heart-shaped brooch. She was enchanted and placed it against her breast. She looked at herself in the mirror. You look very pretty. Of course you do. Beautiful. Bewitching.

Before putting them away, she lingered, turning over the other jewels. She tried on a few more. A necklace, a pearl necklace! In the bottom of the chest was an object wrapped in a cloth. Heavy. Made of metal. She unwrapped it and looked in terror at what was in her hand, an enormous, sticky insect without wings.

Browning 22 was written on the bug.

The pistol of a señorita.

27

And one day Don Xil, who was down in the dumps and seemingly bewitched, left without saying a word and strode purposefully down the long corridor, without caring much if he was seen. Matacáns, ever on the alert, followed him secretly, suspecting some hidden pantry, but surprised all the same at this reckless conduct. Even more so, when the priest headed towards the door that gave on to the vegetable garden and, without looking first, disappeared through the crack in the door. The wretch, thought Matacáns, has discovered another nest and is keeping quiet as a mouse. But, maintaining a safe distance, he observed that the minister was not walking in a straight line, and either was not going anywhere or really did want to shake off anyone who might be on his tail. In fact, judging from his behaviour, Don Xil appeared to be in a daze, oblivious to everything, seemingly without reflexes, dragging his fat bum sluggishly along the narrow paths. Such open territory was not at all to the poacher's liking. He decided to climb up on to a stone wall and settle down into the moss of a salient that served as a viewpoint. What he saw from there made his blood run cold. Camouflaged by the dry bracken, the anarchist of Lousame was lying in wait, ears pinned back, felinely stationed in the exact direction that the mouse was taking, eyes glistening prior to the attack. Don Xil was heading straight for the slaughterhouse and, unable to do anything but keep himself off the menu, Matacáns prepared to be an impotent witness of the implacable laws of nature.

His eyes filmed in slow motion as the anarchist of Lousame described a clean arc and trapped the culprit in his claws. Although used to scenes of hunting, he was horrified at the imminent quartering, a sad requiem for a minister, for in the end he had grown fond of that governor of lives and souls who, deep down, was his own worst enemy. He pictured the libertarian bagpiper ripping out his heart to start with, slowly chewing on the viscera of his sentiments, for revenge is the cruellest stage the mind can invent. Or perhaps not. The cat remained still, holding the priest prisoner, but not looking at him. Perhaps he is plotting something more terrible, something that was practised on those taken out in the war and dumped in the ditches of Néboa: cutting off the victim's balls, while he was still conscious, and stuffing them into his mouth.

But what the cat did was fling the minister into the air and let him fall on the padded lawn. Then he walked off in the direction of the dovecote, miaowing, with his tail at half-mast. It was some time before Don Xil came to.

28

There was going to be a wedding. So Rosa went to Coruña to buy herself a dress and some new shoes. It had been a long time since she had travelled on her own, had almost a whole day to herself. She had left the children with Perellona, a neighbour who knew how to look after them, who was serious and said her prayers. She must be the only one in that parish of braves who did not blaspheme. *For the first drop of milk that Christ drank from his mother's breast!* That was the strongest oath she had heard on her lips. Now, as soon as she boarded the coach, Rosa noticed how strange it was not to have any weight in her hands, an emptiness that freed and disconcerted her. Ever since she had been a child, she had always had to carry something: baskets, legumes, knitting-needles, the iron, the soap for washing clothes, the broom, pots and pans, always something, and then the kids, one after the other on her back. When she went out, the Moses basket, the pram, bags, the worry of the purse which held her keys and cash. She had read in a magazine that King Juan Carlos and Queen Sofía never carried money or keys. Someone walked behind them with change. How lucky they were not to have to worry about that! The world must be divided between those who carry and those who do not carry spare change. She smoothed her hair with her hands. Sighed. Sat back. Her eyes were grateful for the freedom. On the other side of the window, everyone bears a cross. She folded her arms. No, better like this, she let them fall between her legs. I hope no-one decides to sit down next to me.

Why is it that the village is darker? Always light here, in the city. Best off going to the centre. In between large buildings, an empty house with galleries, converted into a dovecote. A pigeon struts on the eaves, swaggers along, pecks furiously at the neck of a female. Mounts her, squeezes her. She suffers in silence. Brute. In the Cantón Gardens, a gardener writes the date in the earth with myrtles. 24 July 1981. The goldfish pond. The monument with the eagle and chains. It says there Concepción Arenal. She helped the prisoners. Who was the other one? Rosalía. That's right, Rosalía de Castro. And the fat one? Cross here, by the Pastor Bank. The fat one was Pardo Bazán. The teacher, Doña Carmen, would add, "Juana de Vega, married to Espoz y Mina, Independence hero, embroidered his flags, stored his heart in a jar of formalin." The Obelisk clock, nearly eleven. Definitely was his heart. It must have turned white. This sun with its smell of salt. The breeze coming from Orzán down Nova Street. All the doors open. A lot of good women in Galicia. Reapers, writers, the hundreds who worked in the tobacco factory. Rosalía angered. Hair in a bun. Teeth clenched. It's a bad tan that comes from harvesting. She can't be wearing anything underneath. Slender. She looks good. One day go to the beach. Take care: fair skin, freckles. She's wearing a lot of make-up. Need time. Wet feet today in the sea if there is time. Good for the varicose veins. The sand tickling your toes, the waves licking the seashore. How lovely. Real Street.

Pascual shop window. Look out of the corner of her eye, reflected between the loose mannequin legs clothed in coloured tights. That blue satin dress. Too forward, very low-cut. She should try it on. Very expensive. Not so expensive. Just this once. Look more. What if someone else takes it? She tried it on. Then she put it back on its hanger. You can't spend money like that, on a whim. She seems to like it as well. Takes a look at it, has another look. Don't let her see you spying. Strange. The two of them look so alike. Anyone would say. Another Rosa. Like twins.

She stopped off at Torreiro, then she went to Barros, and Zara opposite. A lot of people. Good prices. Buy something. That blouse for the summer. That said. Then the summer's over. How nice to browse on her own. You can't with children. Shoes, later. Or not? Santa Catalina Fountain. How about right there, in Madariaga. High heels. I always wanted some, but. The patent leather ones with the gold buckle. Walk slowly, give the foot time to settle. They'd go well with the blue dress. I won't ask if she'll bring the price down. I'll ask. Mum always used to. I'd be embarrassed. I'll take these. So expensive. Wouldn't want them to think. Wouldn't mind going to Bonilla. Chocolate. Too hot. Fat. Potatoes make you fat as well. So do breadcrumbs. Feet red, encased in patent leather.

At the Jesuits' door, a beggar. I've no spare change, maybe I have. The king and queen don't. Poor man, he's lost all his energy. You have to show a little enthusiasm, a bit of feeling, if you're going to beg as well. Carry on, but now you've stopped you have to give something. If only he'd say thank you, God bless you. Nothing. You're a fool. No one gives. You did well to give. Who knows what tomorrow. There's El Pote. We could buy them a set of. Couples nowadays prefer money. Straight into a bank account. Fashions. I don't think that . . .

Cortefiel, on Juan Flórez. That's not bad. Although. You can always try it on. Assistants don't like you trying on. As if they didn't. I should have got the blue one. The prices, of course. That tower, the Alféreces Tower, what a frightening thought to get in the lift. They say it moves when there's a storm. I don't believe it. So much progress. Everyone wants to live in Coruña. He's marrying a girl from Laracha, Cholo's brother. They've a flat in Coruña too, but further out, in Mallos. She works as a cashier in Continente supermarket. With insurance and everything. A uniform like an air hostess'. I wouldn't mind. In Coruña, without animals, without.

When I was small, I wanted to be a hairdresser. Go back for the blue one. On the Obelisk, nearly half past one already. They'll have closed. I'll ask about a discount. Damn, they have closed. My blue dress, in the shop window. That's one good thing. The other, keeps looking, but. Go back in the afternoon.

On Orzán Beach, surfers. In winter, a couple on Lago Beach, in the Camariñas estuary, wearing wetsuits. They were coming out of the water and embraced. The suit clung to her tits and showed off his bulge. They felt, what did they feel? It must be fun, wearing a wetsuit. Riding the crest of the wave, getting feet entangled in the foam, crashing against the sand. The kiss. Television. Both blond, with a dog running after them. Born to play. Clean. Our Trotsky, wouldn't even look at the water. Whimpers, shivers, hides its tail in ugly fashion between its legs. Fleas. Head to tail flea powder. They must have been from Coruña, those surfers. And the ones on their motorbikes with silvery exhaust pipes, and the ramblers with their guitar around the bonfire. City-dwellers, they know how to make the most of the village.

I don't believe it. My blue dress is not there. The other must have come. Bitch. There's one the same. Thank you. I'm not so sure I like it. But.

29

So Don Xil called his companions together and said, "Friends, all of you, I owe you a debt of gratitude which I should like to repay as is fitting, though in the circumstances and condition in which I find myself, I can only make a humble gesture, and I ask you to accept this not for what it is worth but for what it represents." Then he looked at Matacáns with sincere camaraderie, "I owe you most of all, sir, for sticking with me through thick and thin, for ignoring my fiery temper and for lightening the load of my sins; permit me, God, the audacity to bless him, and all the souls in this house." And everyone waited until it was clear that there was no dissent. After Don Xil with emotion untied the knot in his throat, he requested that they follow him to the library.

"They are at your disposal," he said, pointing to a shelf that contained the last books of the ancient illustrated treasure of Arán. "Enjoy!"

"Fine dressing on this paper, Father," said the poacher, who had been waiting to sink his teeth into *The Liberal Ways of Hunting*.

"It's the taste of time, Matacáns. Can't be bought."

The priest, old hunter, incapable now of gnawing, watched nostalgically as the poacher with anxious delight grabbed the haunch of chapter XXIX, "Hares and how to find them", and he was able to read as the letters uncoiled slowly, solitary links of an ancient chain: "In winter, when there is ground frost, you will find them in ploughed fields. Where there is a clearing, they will lie out in the sun."

Mohamed, seeing the melancholic turn the minister had taken, went up to him and said, "There are things in the *Relief for Parish Priests* that I've come across before."

"The world's a small place," said Don Xil.

"A veritable music box."

"I, my Berber friend, only hear the drums of the Last Judgement."

"In Urika, I left behind a brother who whirled round and round in the centre of the universe to the sound of flutes. He said that this would enable him to get to Paradise."

"Do you think there'll be animals in Paradise?" intervened Matacáns, influenced by the matter he held in his hands. "I mean, do you think there'll be hares?"

"I know a man who made that journey," said old Paradela, who had come to gnaw as well. "He was from around Ordes. One night, he didn't come home and, at dawn, they found him frozen by the side of a river. He wasn't breathing or anything. He woke up in the funeral parlour, just as they were about to bury him. He said that he'd been in Heaven and he told the story in such a way that you had to believe him."

"And was there hunting?"

"There must have been. The bit I remember best was when he talked about the Heavenly Banquet. He wasn't joking. He told us things I'd never heard before and certainly hadn't eaten."

"When was this?"

"Round about 1948."

"There was a lot of hunger back then."

"There was indeed."

"And the one you're talking about," asked Matacáns, intrigued, after a silence, "did he actually eat at the Heavenly Banquet or did he just see it, as it were, in a painting."

"No, no, he ate. Besides, where would he have got those recipes from, being a poor fool like myself? Entrecôte steak in a Bordeaux sauce, chestnut ice cream with hot chocolate, hake stuffed with oysters, and something he referred to as spring rolls."

"There can't just have been food!" said Don Xil, somewhat incredulous regarding the stories of the barber Paradela and his friends.

"Even the water tasted better than wine. He swore he was telling us the truth," said the storyteller, crossing his heart. "And Baldario never swore in vain when it came to wine. Another thing that caught his attention were the choirs of angels and of the blessed intoning psalms day and night. The music had them, so to speak, hanging in the air, awake and dreaming at the same time."

"Maybe that was the music my brother could hear," said Mohamed, recalling his dervish relation.

"Why did he come back? Why did Baldario come back?" asked Borborás, staring at Paradela.

"He remembered that he had seen a speck of light at the end of a tunnel, out of which came a voice that commanded, 'Send him back to Galicia, he's not ready yet.' And then the same voice said, 'But give him some time, send him back on a full stomach.' "

The barber declared, "Which just goes to show that God knows how to do the right thing."

30

When Cholo saw Rosa appear at the top of the stairs, he was going to say, You look beautiful, the truth is he thought, I wouldn't mind getting my hands on that, but what he said was, "I've been waiting for an hour, I was going to leave without you". She acted as if she had not heard, went and kissed the children, who were staying with the neighbour. Then she sat in the car, and in order to have somewhere to look she pulled down the mirror on her side and softly combed her fingers through her hair.

At the wedding, in the church, she felt good, as if she had finally found a place in the exchange of glances. She had foreseen the suffering of her feet, which were too thick for her narrow high-heeled shoes, even though she had left them overnight stuffed with wet paper to stretch them a bit. Now she held herself upright, moving her head from time to time with dignity, her hair held in place with a jewel, splendidly attired in pendant earrings and necklace. The heart-shaped brooch sparkling in the hollow of her breasts. There was no-one like her and she knew she was being looked at. But she kept her eyes fixed on the altar, bright, flowery, banked with bunches of daffodils, roses, gladioli, and lots of white, red and variegated carnations. Decorated tastefully. No doubt a woman all the previous afternoon: sweeping the floor, dusting the images, putting out the candles, the flowers. The priest, pale, skinny, four dejected eyes, he had hardly drunk from the chalice, but his voice was different, it must have been because of the microphone that one word pushes another, and he is transformed by the sermon, grows in stature, his withered hands energetic now as he gestures. He is right in what he says. She does not know what she has let herself in for. Tonight, non-stop. Tomorrow's another day. But she looks pretty. She's got character. She had her hair done at Loyra's. She said to me, "If there's no honeymoon, there won't be a wedding. Even if it's in Portugal." Quite right. She might even, who knows? They wanted me to be matron of honour. I said no way.

At the reception, at a restaurant in Pastoriza, Rosa was seated on the top table overlooking the banquet, next to the mother of Nati, the bride. They were farmers. The mother was more nervous than her daughter. She was overcome by such commotion. Her hands crossed on her stomach. She may have been counting. At least two hundred guests. Applause as the bride and bridegroom walk in. Music. Video.

"Nati looks very pretty," said Rosa.

The mother adopted a slightly forced smile. One gold tooth.

"A lot of people."

"Yes."

"Hot, isn't it?"

"Yes."

"Would you like me to hang your jacket up?"

The mother looked at her now sympathetically, as if she had just noticed who was addressing her.

"It's my feet. They're killing me!" she said finally with an open smile.

"Why not take your shoes off?" Rosa encouraged her.

"I don't know whether I should."

"Why not? Who's going to look underneath the table? I think I might take mine off as well."

"When I bought them, I noticed there was . . . But my daughter said no, they look great on you, they look great."

"Where did you get them?"

"In Coruña, Real Street. They cost so much you . . ."

"That's the trouble with weddings, they're so expensive."

"You're telling me!"

"Of course, it's once in a lifetime."

"That's true."

As they were eating, the man with the video camera passed by. The lady with the gold tooth tried to smile. She could not decide, however, what to do with the prawn.

"Nowadays, they photograph everything. I don't know, what with my mouth full!"

"It's fun to look back on though, in a few years."

"Yes, in a few years."

All along the table, the women ended up talking amongst themselves, the men did the same, and the conversations crossed and leaped over heads on the back of wafts and rings of smoke. A tried to get hold of A(1), A(2) or A(n), B the same. Only when the As addressed the Bs, or vice versa, was there a double meaning, in contest, of the type "This filly already has a rider" or "I'd grind that down any day". And, in the game, A had melons, B a turnip. B was the bird that sought flower A, who was also a clam. Meanwhile A drank and B drank more.

When they cut the cake, the As and Bs shouted together, "Kiss the bride, kiss the bride!" One who was bright red stood up and almost choked, "Long live the bride and bridegroom!" Another, "Long live the parents!" And one with a cigar, when everyone had quietened down, "Long live me!" The newly-weds kissed as in a film and Nati's mother pretended to cover her eyes. On top of the cake was a plastic replica of the bride and groom, rigid figures that flew in the air, thrown at random for the single men to fight for; the girls as well, for the orange blossom of the bride's bouquet. Then the friends of the bride-groom went and wrestled with him to cut his tie into small pieces which they kept as trophies. And on came the shouts of *viva!* again, the one with the cigar as well, a "Long live me!" that no-one seconded.

This was followed by the dance. First, the bride and groom danced a waltz. Then, the parents. And the women started joining in, egging each other on in a circle. Rosa watched them with amusement. She smoked. To her right, Cholo was laughing and gesticulating with other men. Gold watch on his wrist, sleeve rolled up. Bruise on the back of his hand. White half moons from telling lies on his fingernails.

"I'm going to dance," she said to the lady.

"Off you go, pet."

She used to love dancing on her own when she was younger, on her own in the disco hall, among sweaty bodies, the music taking her wherever she wanted, her feet in the sand, bubbling, stroking, the foam curling round her toes. And she went and took off her high-heeled shoes again, who cares, and let down all her hair.

"What a surprise! I hadn't seen you."

"I had seen you."

This is Spiderman, who's asking me to dance. I've known him since we were kids, a rascal who'd lift up our skirts at school, always getting into trouble, the best fruit robber in the whole of Arán, that day of the bonfires, up in the peach tree, run, run, old Merantes is here with his stick. The fruit still green, delicious when stolen. A motorbike, as a young man he had a motorbike that would put-put up the street. Fixing the motorbike at the entrance to the disco hall A Revolta, his hands greasy from the wires, are you not coming in? After that he disappeared: embarked. Later in New York, in construction. Tall, skinny, a bag of bones. Aren't those sideburns funny, the white tie and green shirt. Tricoloured shoes just like the ones Negroes wear to dance.

"You're looking very elegant, Antonio," she said, half jokingly.

"There's only one flower here and that's you."

"Stop pulling my leg, go on!"

"Rosa."

116

"Yes."

"Tell me a lie."

"What's that?"

"Tell me you've been waiting for me all these years."

"I've been waiting for you all these years."

"Tell me you'd have died if I hadn't come back."

"I'd have died if you hadn't come back."

"Tell me you still love me as I love you."

"I still love you as you love me."

"Thank you. Thank you very much."

"That was funny! Where did you pick it up, Antonio?"

"In a film. Pretty, isn't it? How's my goddaughter then?"

"Who?"

"The girl, the little one."

"Like a rose."

"Talking of which . . ."

Spiderman rolled back the sleeve on his right arm.

"Look, look what I've got here."

He showed her a tattoo on his forearm. To start with, she recoiled in disgust, but then she took his bare arm and observed it with curiosity.

"A rose and a flag."

"What about this?"

"It's the Irish flag. An Irish American did it for me. Madder than me. He put what he felt like. I said to him, 'Is it pretty? Then I'll have it!' What do I care whether I get one or the other? The rose . . . Don't you think the rose is well done? Apparently it's the rose of Tralee. That's what they call a pretty woman over there. A rose of Tralee."

"You're mad as a hatter. All your life with that there . . ."

"I met a sailor with a tattoo that said: 'Mother, I was born to make you suffer'. Another sailor who had one on his lower abdomen, right here: 'Just for you'."

"Mad as a hatter!"

"But, do you like it?"

"I don't know. Yes."

Spiderman did not stop talking. He was amusing. She could not tell what he was inventing and what he was not. A scatterbrain. She felt good, turning among stories and laughter, but in the end she was the one who said she was tired. She went and sat down next to Cholo. His voice had changed from the drink. While he carried on chatting to his friends, he placed a hand on Rosa's knee.

He caressed her thighs with one hand, while driving with the other. On the way home, oblivious to his blandishments, she watched the slow sequence of Sunday images on the road. Old people sitting on a stone bench, counting cars driving past unusually slowly and well spaced out, the one in front with a surfboard. Figures of women dressed in black, huddled together in a furrow opened by a yoke of cows which a child is pulling along. Earth in wrinkles, earth in the crevices of nails. Earth. Trees dozing in the heat of the day, sleepy pilgrims of the dusk.

A lorry coming the other way.

"Watch out," she said, squeezing her legs together. And finally he took his hand away.

31

Matacáns had learned how to manoeuvre his tail. He gave Don Xil a knock.

"Look down there, on the ground."

At that point the surface twitched, rheums of fresh earth piling up slowly. The two friends watched, absorbed by the phenomenon. Out of the ash-grey heap appeared an emaciated snout sniffing at the emptiness. All they could see apart from that were two blind eyes and a shiny, jet-black skin. It pointed its muzzle in the direction of the two sentinels and seemed not to like the smell, because it withdrew immediately.

"Hey, hey wait!" shouted Matacáns.

The mole reappeared out of the mouth of the recently opened gallery.

"I'm a bit lost. Which way is the vegetable garden?"

"Which way are you coming from?"

"The camellias."

"In that case, you need to carry on a bit. About six strokes."

"I'm afraid I'm in a hurry," the mole took her leave.

"This, madam," said Don Xil with admiration, "is what is called making one's way in life."

"Good God, if it's not the priest!" exclaimed the mole, unable to contain herself on recognizing the voice.

"Do you know me?" Don Xil waited expectantly, raking back in his memory.

"It's the one from Vilachás!" shouted Matacáns for his part, as the penny dropped. "Aroint thee, witch! America the fearless!"

"Shut up, lizard-spiker!"

"Come, come," said Don Xil, still in a state of shock.

"I'll leave you to it," said the mole awkwardly. "Up yours, gentlemen!"

"Wait, America," said the priest in a tone that seemed friendly. "Let bygones be bygones. Let's treat one another as people."

The old fortune-teller listened attentively. Was that not the priest who had roused the mob into burning her house? On the lips of the powerful enemy, such music was an incredible gift.

"See you!" she said.

"Listen, listen," said Don Xil. "You may not believe what I'm going to tell you. Understand it as an act of conscience. I have been given this parenthesis of nature to do justice. The truth, America, is that I always envied you your talent. I had behind me a centuries-old power, a real power, with hierarchy, habit, symbols, books, attributes. And what were you? A poor, lonely woman, a legend between four stone walls."

Matacáns stayed out of the conversation, listening suspiciously. He did not understand very well what was going on. The priest's grovelling struck him as excessive. He himself had been a client of the fortune-teller, but everything in its place.

"And yet," Don Xil continued, "as much as I insisted on distancing you from people with anathemas and threats, the farmers, the humble, those who had lost all hope, they came to you, nor were our cures so different, since you invoked saints and prescribed Hail Marys alongside herbs as well."

America, learned in deciphering the meaning behind words, found nothing this time that sounded like condemnation or censure. What the priest of Arán was saying certainly resembled a confession, an act of wiping the slate clean.

"They trusted you, America."

"That's not entirely true, Don Xil," she said finally. "Don't make them out to be so honourable. They came to you and to me, and they would have gone to the vet or the doctor, had there been one. They knocked at all the doors. They played all the cards."

"Deal me mine!"

"There's no pack, Don Xil. I'm blind."

"What do you know of the world down there? Can one visit the mouth of hell?"

"I don't think so. It's not so bad."

"What's in the foundations of Arán?"

"A graveyard. Bones and more bones."

"And the fortress?" Matacáns now enquired curiously, having decided to take part in the conversation. "They always said there was an ancient treasure."

"Bones!" exclaimed the witch drily.

When they thought she had gone, her head of mourning popped up again.

"Metal: the odd cannon-ball . . . And also some of these."

With her front paws she rolled a small metal disc along the ground.

"A button!" shouted Matacáns, who had rushed forwards to take a look.

"There are thousands. Bones and buttons in the belly of Arán."

"*République française*," Don Xil read in a circle.

"What's that about?" asked Matacáns.

"A battle. Many years ago. The French and the English. They came here to kill each other."

"This is the treasure of Arán!" said America. "See you, gentlemen! I'm off to find some worms."

32

"Her name is Beatriz," said Toimil to the king of Galicia. "She's fun and a little bit fat, rosy cheeks like dahlias. Chestnut-brown eyes with a dash of green. A washerwoman's hands."

"I like that romance," said His Majesty.

"Albar took him to her, I told him where to go. She was picking wild strawberries by the river, while she kept an eye on the cattle. He was wearing his Prussian riding jacket and whistling, with that contraption in his ears. They met where the water flows back and the alders drink day and night. She stopped him as he was going past."

"What did she say?"

"She asked him if he would lend her his walkman. There's no love without music. The two of them sat down in the field, joined by the musical thread, while Albar, discreetly, nibbled clover in amongst violets and chrysanthemums. She mouthed the words slowly. *Ah, how cruel is the heart.*"

"What's that then?"

"Mexican. From the other world."

"Of love?"

"Breaking up."

"These songs about falling out of love are the ones that make people fall in love," said the king of Galicia.

And that was how Simón of Arán met Beatriz of Grou, in the country of the Rio Grande. The morning of the following Sunday he stopped by the same place as if he just happened to be going that way, though his eyes told a different story, and she laughed so much when she saw him that she made him go red and look away. Beatriz, noticing that he was upset, meek ox lowering head in the light of a snub, went and stroked Albar's neck and twirled his mane, curling it with her fingers.

"I bet you don't take me for a ride."

This was not foreseen. A bird flapped savagely in the cage of Simón's chest. It pecked furiously at his Adam's apple, up his throat. Simón looked at Beatriz in amazement. So fresh. Challenging. Pulling his leg.

"I bet you don't dare."

Happy fear. Joyful premonition. Beak, now fist.

"Oh, go on! Only as far as the old mill. And back."

He almost choked. Now it's there, neither coming out nor going back down, a fistful of flesh with feathers stuck in his throat.

"I bet you don't do it."

The robin flew out of his throat and landed on the blackberry bush. Simón followed it with his eyes, relieved. A robin pecks at blackberries. He turned to face the girl. Eyes to die for.

"Come on," she said.

She put her arms around his waist. Albar made a half-turn and caracoled away.

33

The cold water from the tap rinsed off the foam and raised purple patches on her skin. Washing away the watercolour of blood, Rosa looked at her ring finger. As she turned it around, the gold ring shed its light on the reddened skin. She tried moving it gently, but could not get it past her knuckle, caught as it was in the folds of flesh. She pulled harder. At the point where it had been for years, since the wedding, it had left a mark white as bacon. Rosa wanted to slide it over her wrinkles but had to give up in some discomfort. She returned the ring to its place and then tried with one sharp tug to see if it would slip off, but it was in vain. What had started as an unconscious movement had become an obsessive struggle to beat the fat and the folds of skin. She slid the ring back down her finger. Heaps of greasy years. Her hand wasn't that fat. Or was it? She felt her waist, her bottom. She gave her double chin a pinch. It wasn't that fat. Or was it?

She smeared her finger with soap, in particular where the ring was. Their willies. It's incredible how they stretch and shrink, how they swell with just one stroke, one rub, up and down and that's it, up they go, anxious to penetrate. He liked it when she cupped his balls in her hand. When they were young, they never stopped. In the past they were always touching each other. When they walk around in bare feet, the little birdie shrivels to nothing. She tried again. She went slowly, softly, pulling and turning at the same time, in a spiral. When the ring passed the fibre of her knuckle, Rosa put her inflamed finger under the tap to feel the childlike relief of the water. Then she looked at the inside of her wedding ring. It was brighter. When a cry brought her back to the world, she went and placed the ring on the sill of the open kitchen window, on the white tile, without spotting a thieving magpie in the fig tree. Twelve years she'd been married now. It didn't take long to say it. When she left, the long-tailed bird saw an open sky. A kleptomaniac of pretty trinkets.

34

The 300 crows of Xallas alighted on the roof of the manor house.

Rosa sensed death as well, in the silence crouching between the caws of the crows, but she did not want to see it. From time to time, she would go outside and search the fields of the manor house in vain for the solitary figure in black with its woolly flock, or the squalid trickle of smoke stretching out of the chimney-top, or at least the monologue of a single item on the clothes-line. That is all Misia's presence had been in recent times. Dressed in mourning, her face almost completely obscured by a Portuguese scarf, steering the white and nervous docility of her sheep. An elusive shadow with an armful of firewood among the chestnut trees. Someone hanging out socks where the clothes-line has fallen. On the few occasions they did meet, she appeared evasive, frightened like her sheep. She talked to herself. One day she stopped, leaning on a staff, and gave her a strange look. "Who is it? Is that Rosa?" Very sad.

All day long Rosa felt anxious, a presentiment cawing at her insides. At nightfall, when Simón came home, she could not resist any longer and she went round to the house. The front door was locked. She rapped on the knocker, the ball of the world in a fist, cold iron fingers. Then she called out for the lady, slowly, without making too much noise, she did not want to frighten her. Perhaps she is in bed, ill, with a fever, driving away the mad thoughts from her head. Or perhaps not. Maybe she's watching me through the keyhole or from behind the veil of the lace curtain. Nothing. Nor is there light on the other side.

In the evening, she did not voice her suspicions in front of her husband. What do you want to stick your nose in there for? That's what he would say. But partly also in rebellion against this strange power of seeing ahead of time, of discerning the sinister side of things. She thought that each time she expressed her fears, her premonitions, her obsessions, each time she put her thoughts into words, her predictions finally came true. She was afraid of herself, of her own head, of that unhealthy tendency to turn every event into a sign, a warning, a message, in such a way that life was an anguished and unending fable, in which tiny, invisible threads joined the fate of things and of people. Sometimes, when she was concentrating on the job in hand, sewing or ironing or in the kitchen, her head would go off on its own, shoot down the tunnel of her eyes, a convoy of beads and feelings rolling quickly, jolting noisily, turning into words that spilled over, until an insignificant detail appeared in her way. A shadow. And the brakes gave a deafening screech. And there they were, back in the same station.

The following day, the 300 crows of Xallas were still perched on the roof of the manor house.

"Poking your nose into other people's business," is what her husband said.

Her head of course knew it all, but it could not leave her alone. Better if it stopped thinking. If it deceived her.

"We should go and have a look. She hasn't been out in days. She hasn't even let the sheep out."

"She'll have gone!"

"We should go and see. She's an old woman. She has no-one."

"She's mad! She's like a witch!"

"Just have a look."

"Look, look! And what are we going to look at? Didn't you say it's all locked up?"

You have to knock the door down, says her head, which is slowly paving the way. Or through a window.

He would have preferred it if she had adopted a different tone, so that he could carry on refusing. He felt anger towards everything that came from that large house, be it splendour or ruin, ancestry or misery, the cursed vice of the stone oozing history, that blasted centre of the universe. We'll have to go and have a look then. When she uses that voice, she knows what she's saying. A sixth sense. Frightening.

Cholo went to the granary and released the house dog.

"Come on, Trotsky." The mutt was going crazy when it reached the front door. Excited barks interspersed with a wounding lament. It was dying to go in, dying at the same time to take to its heels. It dragged its body behind its snout along the door-stone, panting nervously. Suddenly, it recoiled in horror, its tail shrivelled to nothing between its legs. The man tried to lever the door open with a crowbar.

Locked. Barred and everything.

"I'm going round the back," said Cholo. "Through the vegetable garden." The door there was semi-rotten.

Rosa noticed her heart beating in the shell of her ear when she leant against the door. Then, the unhesitating blows of her husband on his own round the back, the groaning of the old wood clinging obstinately to the rusty arms of the hinges, the hysterical barking of the dog as it enters the house, chasing her heart from the shell.

Cholo removed the bar and looked outside. Pale. Agitated. "You'd better not go in."

"Move out of the way."

Goaded by the dog's painful howls, some of the sheep were trying to come round by pathetically straightening their wobbly knees. Most of them lay motionless, on the other side of the line of agony, around the lady's body, a beggar's corpse, huddled on a piece of sacking at the foot of the stairs.

"There were mice sniffing about," said her husband uneasily. "Enough to make you sick. Terrible."

"Go on, go and get a blanket," said Rosa, as she crossed herself.

35

Through the chink in the ceiling, Don Xil watched the procession: Rosa, Simón, the old people in the village and the 300 crows.

"Not much of a funeral for a lady," said the barber Paradela. "In the old days, she'd have had 300 wailing mourners who, they say, accompanied one Formoso of Viana."

"Quick, sir, quick!" the poacher burst into the funereal belvedere. "Eight eggs and a gold ring!"

"Gold?" enquired the barber sardonically. "Of the kind that comes out of a Moor's arse, if you'll pardon the expression."

"No, it's genuine!" said Matacáns. "And there are eight green speckled eggs!"

"Where is the treasure?"

"A magpie's nest at the top of a willow tree!"

"Take me to the long-tailed bird, Matacáns, so that it can gouge my eyes out!" exclaimed Don Xil, emerging from his depression.

"Not so fast, sir."

"This is the end of the house of Arán, friends. I've seen enough paintings! In these parts, dying is an art."

"Truth to say, death is a vice in this country," declared Paradela.

"It's the air in this house," said Mohamed suddenly, having remained deep in thought in one corner. "It has particles of sadness. Like breathing the mist of an ancient sea."

"A marsh, you might say, a foggy swamp!"

And the barber says, "A den of mice even."

"We must sprout wings!" said the poacher.

> *"At the top of the willow tree there's a nest*
> *with a treasure: one gold ring and eight green eggs!"*

"I've had enough, Matacáns. I'm off to gnaw the foundations of this graveyard. Better still, I shall lie down to distil nostalgia. Fade away in the old style. And goodbye!"

"It's the air," repeated Mohamed. "A sad chemistry. It sits on the lungs like lichen."

"Is there no cure?"

"Of course there is! A change of air!"

"Come on, Don Xil, let's make a pilgrimage!"

"It hardly seems possible," said the minister, as if reminded of an old vow, "never to have visited San Andrés!" This invocation seemed to revive everyone's spirits: "San Andrés de Teixido, the sanctuary at the end of the earth! If you don't go when alive, you must go when you have died!"

"But if I go," said Don Xil finally, "who will stay behind in this graveyard? No, friends, you go. God won't release me. I shall never leave Arán."

As much as they insisted, they could not get him to change his mind. They started out on their merry pilgrimage, but regretted having to leave him behind.

"They all went," Toimil recounted to the king of Galicia, "except for the poor priest. And that is when the manor house started to burn, as if the fire had waited lurking among the embers on the hearth and leaped out, like a snake's tongue, as soon as it saw that it was alone. An enormous bonfire illuminated the night of Arán. No one did anything to extinguish it, though some shadows were seen to creep out with belongings, carpets and furniture. Rosa approached the façade. The unrestrained flames burst the windows and ran from side to side, clinging to the back of the wind. They flickered mockingly on her face. In these parts, my lord, God paints like a furious romantic artist."

36

And Rosa took the children up a hill to find the mimosa wood, since she was fond of the first flower to light up in winter. The eldest, who was in front, disappeared down a path and came running back in a state of excitement, saying that there was an animal lying on the ground but still alive, with a fierce face, which had bared its teeth, very big, a wolf or something like that.

"A dog maybe," said Rosa, laughing. And she picked up a stick and added in amusement, "Let's go see that monster, hoy, hoy!"

"Really, Mum, there is," said the child, getting upset, as his mother pulled aside the branches of broom that covered the path. "And it's not a dog."

No, it was not.

"You see, Mum!"

"Stay where you are!" she said, gripping the stick defensively.

With painful ferocity, the animal laboured to open its mouth, revealing the threat of yellow teeth and black gums. Squalid, bones pressing against dirty skin, sweaty with tufts of sticky, earth-clotted hair, speckled with bits of dry bracken, all the life that was left spoke through its eyes. In their glimmer, Rosa saw something that made her away.

"It's a fox," she said. "Half dead."

Around it, the grass and crushed branches revealed a long, desperate struggle. One of its back legs was caught in a trap, but the other, which was more visible, enmeshed in the wire, had been badly cut, as if the animal had broken it while wrestling to free itself from the trap. The gashes had formed pustules and where the iron had made an incision there oozed blood full of pus. Only the tail remained soft and lucid, as if it wanted to separate from the scabby root one day soon and make off through the air like a sprightly squirrel. The initial surprise had given way to an unbearable stench; Rosa sought out the life in those wild, resentful, human eyes.

"Poor thing!" said Rosa. And then, nervously, "We'd better go."

The animal made a huge effort to close its mouth and dropped its head down on to the bed of leaves in languid foreshortening, oblivious to the movement of the child who advanced holding a stick out like a goad. Rosa pulled him back brusquely.

"Leave it alone!"

"I want to see if it bites the stick."

"Come on, let's go!"

In the last look she gave the prostrate body, she noticed the agitated breathing in the bellows of its ribs.

"Is it going to die, Mummy?" asked the girl.

"Of course it is, stupid," said the boy.

Very quietly, in the golden wood of acacias, Rosa gathered branches with which to adorn the house. Not so the children, who leaped about noisily, fighting to pick the ones with most flowers, mad creatures, how lucky they were the way they forget.

On their return, on emerging from the cart-track that leads to the road, they heard the sound of boredom rolling along the asphalt. It was Spiderman, with his hands in his pockets, kicking an empty Coca-Cola can. Before Rosa had a chance to say hello, the children ran to tell him what they had seen. There was a fox caught in a trap, in the pine forest, and it was dead, half dead, still alive, but its legs were badly wounded. So he said, "Let's go and have a look." And they went with him without asking their mother for permission, "It's ours, it's ours!"

"Of course it's yours!" Spiderman was saying. "Was it you who found it? Then it's yours."

Rosa was arranging the mimosas in a vase on the kitchen sill, doing it without thinking, enchanted by the splendour of the vegetal jewel, when she heard the house dog's demented barking. She knew what was coming next. And she closed her eyes before going to the front door.

"It's a female!" Spiderman proclaimed.

37

And one day Beatriz said to Simón, "Do you know how to get to Grou?" She said it in a fun way, as was her nature, and he interpreted it as an invitation. But it was a challenge. "To get to Grou, you have to pass through three rings. One is silver and the other two are gold. When you arrive and you see the great sow, give it something it will like. If it lets you continue, you'll meet the grandfather of grandfathers. You'll have to conquer him." And then Bea turned a somersault and disappeared. She used to perform this trick and, after vanishing, she was still heard to laugh for a moment with a blackbird's voice among the alders.

Saturday evening, Simón prepared all the finery for himself and for Albar, who observed the fripperies of the festal attire destined for him with some resignation. In the barn, sitting on a log at the horse's feet, the man barely slept as he polished the belts, the saddle and his own boots, finally collapsing on a truss of hay. Albar woke him early so that he had time to wash and to prepare himself as field marshal in the tradition of the Ulla carnivals. He was thirsty that morning, a strange need in his mouth. He drank a pitcher of good milk, pearl drops slipping down the felt of his beard, until he mopped them up with the back of his hand. He harnessed Albar, adjusted the blue Prussian riding jacket with scarlet pocket flaps and felt the hilt of his hussar's cutlass, for it was a great day of love and challenges.

Morning had broken in Arán to the symphony of goldfinches and high up, with starry song, a skylark took the place of the polestar. The other members of the household were fast asleep when Albar cut a caper on the threshing floor and trotted off with the field marshal at the reins, village alarm clock the hoofs echoing against the paving stones of the narrow streets. Man and beast still had time to stop at the Scallop Fountain and to drink at length from the tap.

Lost further on in the same mist that had settled in the river valley, they realized that they were caught up in the first challenge, which was that of a silver ring. The fog was so thick that its glistening threads hung from their eyelashes like lace curtains and the world was obscured from view. Simón was just thinking how disturbingly dark a white cave can become when Albar took the decision to follow the course of the river, and this is how they reached the ruins of the fulling-mill, which was where the long sheet of mist was being woven in melancholic linen. Having gone past the old factory where the river sang ancient ballads in the mill-leats, they saw the heron clearly now, which gave a blue hue to the birch which whitened its wings.

Simón was very taken up gazing at the illustration of his loved one in the book of his innermost thoughts when he had to come to his senses, because Albar spun round in discomfort. They were, so to speak, stuck in a basket, the wood of acacias had closed in thickly around them. As if they had all lit up at once, the candles illuminated the beadlike fronds of a flowery carnival. Held back by the vegetation, Simón was still fascinated by the pristine gold of that cathedral. Albar was more worried about how to get out of there, irritated by the treacherous embrace of the wild acacia that hides its spikes under a purple chasuble. To carry on like this would have been a torment. To turn around would have meant going over past suffering. This time it was the man who took the initiative. Simón dismounted and no sooner had he unsheathed the cutlass than the nastiest branches in their grotesque masks withdrew stealthily, clearing a path down which they advanced with great composure.

They then arrived at a belvedere where the second gold ring was immediately revealed to them: a vast field of gorse with flowers resplendent and spines like daggers surrounded what was undoubtedly Grou, raised like an ancient fortress, a settlement huddled in a circle with concentric walls between which cattle grazed and kitchen gardens grew. A cart-track sprang up at their feet and Albar, in wary fashion, distrustful of the flowers with spiny soul, decided to take the easy path and received no order to the contrary from the reins. But what happened was that the more ground they covered, the more remote they found themselves, and it made little sense, because the Barbanzan's goal was Grou and that was the direction the path seemed to take, a mirage. Time passed, the lance of the angelus sun piercing man and beast, and all they did was to go round in circles inside a maze that took them further away from the village and made the plumes of smoke holding the vacuous balance appear unreal.

Albar was beginning to get fed up and Simón to despair, struggling to do away with the vile thought that love is always a bitter fruit, when the gallant fixed his gaze on them, on the columns of smoke, and realized that not only were they not moving, but they were exactly the same colour as the stone of the scene in which they stood. And the same was true of the other forms: the pensive donkey remained eternalized, the cows and sheep locked in the kiss of the grass, the old woman in the window glued to the gnomon of the sundial. The spell was enough to send you mad, because if you threw a stone, which Simón did as soon as he dismounted, it bounced across the sky as pebbles do on the salty sea when thrown by a lover. That world was a kind of bubble, a sibyl's crystal ball, placed on a lunar hill and girdled by a ditch of green water and that long, insurmountable defence of the ring of golden gorse. Simón felt like a moth, banging uselessly against the lamp of desire. And his powerlessness to conquer the charm gradually turned into a rage that finally burst forth in a howl that echoed painfully down the corridors of the sky and stunned even the sedate Albar. He opened the book of his innermost thoughts at the illustration of his loved one and summoned all the air inside his chest. At what followed, the whole of nature shuddered. Simón vomited up a piece of meat like a heart. And then he called out her name – "Beatriz!" – in a shout of conjuration that creaked through the ancient doors. That world began to move, the village brake was released, the smoke wound up in the form of a turban, the old woman in the window emptied the dirty water from the washbasin into the sun, and the mazelike path unfurled like a weaver's loose knot.

38

"Spiderman carried it on a sort of stretcher," Toimil informed the king of Galicia, "followed by the children, who were very excited. Rosa came to the door to meet the procession, her hands folded in her apron, unsure what to do, afraid of approaching."

"Look, it's a fox," he was saying, as eager as the kids were. His sleeves were rolled up, revealing hairy forearms.

"But . . . listen!"

"It's ours, it's ours!" the children chorused.

"But . . . what were you thinking of?"

She had the sensation that the whole world was watching, spying on that novelty, laughing at that peculiarity, a dying fox, the stench of death from the woods, there on the threshing floor.

"It'll get better, you'll see," he said in encouragement.

What a madman is this, she thought. She said, "It stinks!"

"I'll wash it, you'll see. Bring some warm water."

"Water?"

"Warm water. And soap."

He laid it down on the threshing floor very carefully. The animal, feeling the solid ground beneath it, tried to get up, fleeing anxiously with its head, but only managed to drag itself a few inches on its front legs. It let out a whimper, shuddered, and finally half-closed its eyes in submission, dropping its head and staring along the ground, oblivious to the expectant crowd, and the huge, human eyes exploring each beat of its ruin.

"But . . ."

"Bring some water in a tub. Then we'll wash this young lady down a bit."

As he said it, without looking at Rosa, he placed his hand very slowly on the back of the fox's neck, "There, girl, gently does it." When he stroked the stiff hair behind its ear with his fingertips – "There, girl, that's it" – the animal suddenly made as if to bite him, but was pulled back by the pain and mouthed in agony, the man's hand placed on the spot where the male would normally nuzzle its teeth.

With Rosa and the kids watching on, Spiderman very gently washed the pustules on its legs and the scab on its behind. Where the trap had caught and the wire had cut, where there were gashes and blackened blood, also seemed to be the least sensitive part, and the fox let him work without complaining, "There we are, poor thing, everything's broken."

They left the fox in the sun while it was still up, Spiderman keeping an eye on the dogs that had smelled it out and were circling, growling, alerted by the furious barking of Trotsky underneath the granary. Rosa had still not grown used to the idea when he said that it was very weak and they had to get it to eat something, following that with the bold suggestion that they find it a safe place away from the night frost.

"But . . ."

"Please, Mummy! Please, Mummy!"

"A shed or something, I'll look after it."

She was going to say, This devil of a man, how interfering! But she said, "We'll see what Cholo thinks when he gets home."

But it was too late when the man of the house returned; there was no-one to tell him the story of the fox.

39

So it was easy enough arriving in Grou, everything forgotten now, happily, Simón and Albar urged on by the psychometric sounds of the earth, that manner of roaring that comes about on Sundays. But before entering the main street, they saw a colossal pig in front of them, which was sticking its snout into some pots of geraniums without being reprimanded by a single human being. As soon as it saw the strangers, man and beast, the sow ran after them, grunting, its little eyes popping stupidly out of its brutal head. Simón had never seen anything like it, nor had Albar, judging by the jump he gave. Squat, its teats trailing along the ground, it was, however, as broad as an ox. With a malicious look, it blocked the path, remaining impassive before the impatient snorts of the steed. Women's heads began to appear at the windows.

"You've got to throw it something!" shouted one.

"Throw it something!" they all chorused.

The huge sow stood demanding and scornful at the customs point in the street.

"It has to be something it likes."

"It doesn't like maize bread!"

"No chestnuts!"

And then Simón went and very solemnly opened his haversack and produced a bloodstained cloth tied at the four corners. He undid it slowly, making sure the pig could see. The pig drooled greedily. There was expectation at all the windows of Grou. Simón took the bloody muscle and weighed it in the plate of his hand. Everyone watched as it fell in slow motion at the feet of the large sow.

"A heart!" said the murmur as it turned into a shout of surprise in the mouths of the village. "He's thrown it a heart!"

The pig, half given to gluttony and half in amazement, looked around and promptly devoured it in one bite, blood dripping from its jaws. It then moved aside and marched off, snuffling with its head bowed.

"It sure liked that!"

Simón looked to his right. He was being addressed by a bearded old man, virtually a dwarf, with a red sash tied around his waist. He had pointed ears and a glint in his eye.

"That's the grandfather of grandfathers!" the woman in the window nearest him explained respectfully.

"Now, wait just a moment," he said pensively, twirling his beard, "what goes along the ground but never sits down?"

Everyone turned and looked at Simón. So much silence began to hurt him. He knew the answer, groaning at the gates of memory, bringing all the dry leaves, but found he could not speak, still consumed by the price of a heart ripped out to state the name of his loved one. He thought of using his hands, but it was no use, whatever it was slipped through his fingers.

Everyone had given up on him.

"The wind!" Albar suddenly said.

The old man was quite taken with this way of answering the riddle through the horse's mouth. The women crossed themselves.

"I was wondering where you were," said Beatriz at the end of the street.

The large sow rubbed its belly against the doorpost. From its snout hung a slobber of violets. Inside, it was all compliments. Beatriz had three fawning, gregarious aunts, short and a little bit fat, who wore green and red skirts, and who presented Simón, feeling small behind the large pine table, with a wide range of the earth's fruits, among other dishes they gave him some of the local buttery breast-shaped cheese freshly wrapped in a cabbage leaf, waffles sprinkled with caster sugar, blood pancakes with choice honey and a Holy Year red, followed by a herb liqueur to bless it all.

And there they came, red-faced and smiling, to ask Simón if he wanted more and if he was comfortable. And he, with rosy cheeks, would respond with his mouth full to such attentions.

"I told you he doesn't speak," Beatriz warned them.

"I know, dear, but that doesn't mean we can't ask him anything," replied the one who answered to the name of Aunt María.

"He's a well-built lad," said Aunt Maruxa.

"And he has such a gentle face," added Aunt Marisa, pleased at how much their guest was eating. "He looks like a nice boy."

"Whenever I hear anything like that," said a booming voice suddenly from the bench by the hearth, "whenever I hear anyone spoken to like that, I get the impression they're being called stupid."

"Uncle Roque!" shouted Beatriz.

"You're so rude!"

"Always back to front!"

"Hee, hee, hee."

The one laughing with impish malice stirred the embers with a poker and a swarm of sparks rose towards the chimney's black hole. His face was half shaded by an emigrant's hat. A blackbird pecked in the breadlike clarity of the window.

"As far as being mute goes," said Uncle Roque, unperturbed, "I understand that it's curable so long as the mute has an ear. All you have to do is cut off the tip of his tongue."

"Oh, stop it!"

"With a single chop. A countryman told me this in Cuba. He had a parrot that would say, 'Galician dirty paws, Galician dirty paws!' Hee, hee, hee."

"Drink and shut up!" Aunt María cut him short.

"Don't take any notice of him," said Bea, smiling at Simón. "He doesn't mean it. I think it's the smoke from the hearth that goes to his head. He hasn't moved from that corner since he came back."

"He always was a stirrer!" said Aunt María, who had a hand in everything. "He was an old know-it-all even when he was young. A stubborn little boy!"

From his corner, the old man winked conspiratorially at the guest and then began to sing softly, dragging his voice along like the axle of a cart.

> *"I have fleas in my shirt,*
> *I have lice in my underwear.*
> *But I've cows in my shed*
> *— the neighbours are not unaware!"*

"Go ahead, sing!" Aunt María laughed despite herself.

"He came back poorer than when he went!"

"He brought a hat with him!"

"And a pipe!"

"And a shirt with a palm tree embroidered on it!"

"Enough, enough."

"Eat some more, boy."

"He can't."

"What do you mean, he can't? He's plenty of room."

"Just a little more."

"And after the meal," Toimil told the king of Galicia, "the two of them went on a lovers' outing on the back of Albar and came to a deep blue lake, as if the sky had collected in a china bowl in which the woollen brushstrokes of the lazy clouds were sharply reflected on that day of recreation."

And it was true that the delicate landscape which contained them, the horse and also a crow perched alone in a bare tree, had a certain hard gleam to it, since the lake had formed in the open cavity of an abandoned kaolin mine, as was apparent from the white fringe bordering the waters in which the high vault shimmered. The sun grew cold where they were and, in horror, as if the simple crack of a bone could break it all, they watched the pair of swans glide over the varnish of silence.

"That's right, my lord," said Toimil, "the loyal Maeloc and the lady of Normandy have been using the abandoned mine since they were fired at and had to leave the lake in Xuño."

40

When Rosa opened, having heard a knock, Spiderman was at the door with the morning dew on his leather boots and she said, "Oh, it's you." And then, "Do you want to come in?" And he said that well, he would not mind a coffee, if it was not too much bother.

"And your husband?"

"He's left."

"What did he say?"

"Nothing, I haven't even had time to tell him."

Rosa went into the kitchen and found a saucepan. She had not tied her hair up. She had bags under her eyes. A lazy gait, of slippers.

"I brought it something," Spiderman said. "Some aspirin."

"Aspirin?"

"If they're good for people, they'll do for foxes as well. And this is a cream my mother had when she cut herself on the sickle. Did you go and see how it was?"

"No way! This whole thing is madness. I can't even bring myself to go up to the door."

"What about the children?"

"They wanted to, sure enough. I sent them off to school a short while ago. The little ones are asleep. They were just about ready," she said with a tired smile.

"I was like that as well. Out like a light as soon as the cock crowed."

"Their sleep's all up-ended."

"Why don't you give them some herbs, some lime tea or something?"

"That's what I need. I think if they let me, I'd sleep for the rest of my life. I'd get into bed and stay put."

She placed a cigarette in her mouth, breathing in after the sigh. He hurriedly felt in his pocket for the lighter.

"I don't think you ever fully recover from not sleeping at night," Spiderman said. "I would always go to my parents' bed. I'd nestle in beside my mother, but not sleep. There were nights when the moon was out and the figures on the curtains would be drawn on the ceiling and on the walls. Birds that stretched out in shadows and things like that."

Rosa looked him in the face for the first time, grateful for the confidence, and saw the shadow play in his eyes on a moonlit background. Men did not talk like that.

"But the bit I enjoyed most was in winter. I'd huddle up to her, curl up underneath the blankets, and listen on the one side to her breathing and on the other to the wind moaning outside, howling around the rooftop."

Tell me more, she was going to say, but she extinguished her cigarette and said, looking out over the threshing floor, "It's getting late."

"So it is," he said, standing. "Will you give me a plate with some milk?"

When she gave it to him, he dropped in the aspirin and stirred the milk with his finger to soften them up so that they would dissolve.

"I'm going to see how the young lady is. Are you coming?"

"I will, if you go first."

"OK."

Spiderman carefully pushed the door of the shed, which still creaked, painfully opening an accordion of light. Eyes and teeth gleamed for a moment, signs of life on the sacking. The animal appeared small on the ground while the human figures grew to extraordinary sizes on the screen of the door.

"Let's have a look at you, precious," said Spiderman, as he leant down and placed the plate near the fox's snout. Then, very gently, he rubbed ointment into the wounds. On feeling the contact, the animal tried to move, but could only emit a soft whimper, like a dog beaten into submission. It laid its head down, gazing into the darkness, oblivious to the light of the milk.

"It won't eat if we're here," said Rosa.

"No. And it must be starving hungry."

When they came out, they were happily blinded by a renascent sun. Spring pulsated in the air. At the side of the house, next to the fig tree, the elder blossomed with white butterfly wings, vegetal flakes emerging along the stalk from their winter niche.

Spiderman yawned and stretched his arms. A gold cross hung on the wolf's chest. Excuse me. Rosa laughed.

"It's a beautiful day," he said.

"It'll soon get cold. In the evening."

"If you don't mind, I'll stick around so that I can have another look later. If you don't mind."

"Now, what would I mind for!"

"I could always, if you wanted, I could always do something," he said cautiously.

"Don't talk nonsense! What could you do?"

"Well, I could cut some wood or . . ."

"We've wood to last us years. My brother . . ."

"Is the roof leaking?"

"No, no," she said with amusement. "Not yet."

"I could, I could paint the front of the house." And he pointed to the faded white walls of the house. Rosa could see what was wrong as well, scars blackened by the damp, the lines of stone obstinately reappearing underneath the cement.

"What do you mean, paint!"

149

"You bet I will!"

"Don't talk nonsense!"

"What colour do you want it?"

"Stop pulling my leg."

"Then, how about some flowers?"

"Flowers?"

She could not tell why, but she felt a stab of pain in her insides. She looked around in confusion. It was true. Apart from the wild white of the elder, there were no flowering plants. In the kitchen window, the cut mimosas twinkled and overlapped.

"That's right, flowers. Why not?" said Spiderman. He was going to add, This is something I do not understand, why houses here do not have a garden, flowers at each corner, only the dead have them. But he kept quiet. Said, "That's right, you'll see. It's easy. I'll make some window boxes out of logs and put one at either end. Even if it's only geraniums. And around the threshing floor I'll stick in some hydrangeas. It'll look pretty, you'll see."

"The animals will eat them."

"Not these, they won't. They're very bitter."

"Well, if you must. The truth is I've often thought, but . . ."

"It's to keep me amused. From time to time, I'll check on the animal, and potter around."

She went towards the door. Flowers. A garland of flowers for her thoughts. Before entering, she said, "I heard you were leaving."

"Yes, well. I'm not sure yet."

Spiderman looked in the barn for the tools, and then found some wood. He would make two long window boxes, the timber supported by struts in the shape of a cross, just as he had seen them made abroad one time. Mental notes for an impossible hearth. Pucho Boedo's song: "Whoever put in your genes the wanderlust of the knife grinder?" His mother, the last tie. Dead now.

During the morning, Rosa listened to the monotonous growl of the saw, broken at intervals by the crisp carillon of the hammer. These sounds suited the house, as if they had always been there, challenging the others that lengthened the silence: the cistern, the shutter pounded by the invisible wind, the arachnid explosion of a piece of plastic in the rubbish bin.

Spiderman knocked at the door and she hastened to see what he had completed, but he brought the empty plate.

"It ate everything," he said. "I think I might get it some meat."

"But . . ."

"It's a good sign, you know?"

"Hang on, stay where you are. I've some chicken in the kitchen."

"OK. Raw. Chopped into pieces. I'll do it, if you'll lend me a knife. God knows what the poor animal's insides must be like!"

There he was in the kitchen, sleeves rolled up, hands bloodied by the meat. Would you mind showing me that tattoo again? What nonsense!

"Oh, and I made a window box. Go and have a look, if you want."

When the kids came back from school, the fox was lying on the sacking in the sun, outside on the threshing floor, with its eyes half-closed, and Spiderman sitting next to it, watchful, a stick in his hand ready to drive away the dogs that were circling.

"Is it better?"

"Not yet, poor thing. But do you know something, something very important? It ate, it ate like a queen."

"What did it eat?"

"Chicken, a breast of fresh chicken."

"And crisps?" asked the girl. "Do foxes eat crisps?"

"Don't be stupid," said the boy. "Foxes don't eat crisps. They're carnivorous!"

"So what? Trotsky eats crisps."

"That's enough, now. I don't think it'd like crisps, but you never know."

Spiderman then approached the kids, who were squatting on the ground, as if about to share a secret.

"You see this finger, the one that doesn't have a nail?"

They could see it. The middle finger of the right hand ended in a stump and, with a third of it amputated, looked odd between the index finger and the ring finger. Spiderman waggled it about and the children stared in amazement.

"It's missing a piece, you see? Poor thing. It got eaten by a fish."

The children grimaced, as if they could hear the gnawing of teeth.

"Piranhas. Have you heard of piranhas?"

"Once, on TV," said the boy, "they ate a horse in one minute."

"Well, they ate this piece of my finger."

"Did it hurt?" asked the girl. "I mean, did it hurt a lot?"

"I don't know. I don't remember. To tell the truth, it wasn't piranhas, that was a joke. It was an iron monster."

After a silence, the three of them turned and looked at the animal.

"Do you think it'll be our friend when it's better?"

"I'm sure it will."

"Like a dog? Will it play with us like a dog?"

"Let's come to an arrangement. How about we let it go back to the hills?"

They fell silent. They did not seem to like this idea very much.

"It'll remember you. At night, it'll watch the light in your house."

"What if we leave? Mummy wants to leave for Coruña."

At that point, Rosa appeared at the door with the baby in her arms and called them in for lunch.

"Mummy, Mummy!" the girl shouted. "Did you know, piranhas tore off a piece of Spiderman's finger?"

"It was an iron monster," said the boy.

Rosa stood watching him. "Why don't you come in as well?"

41

And one Sunday that had dawned grey and with drenched feet, Simón went to Grou to visit his loved one. But he noticed something strange – what is called a presentiment – because the whole of nature was quiet and sorrowful, the morning mist dripping down the frayed edges of the frowning trees. In the grief of the hedges, a stonechat tried not to sing, disguised as a sparrow. All the creatures seemed destined for a distant place that was not their own, as if forewarned by the earth. A drone flew aimlessly over the uniform petals of sadness. A slug slid down the parchment of granite with the eternal nostalgia of animals that are without a shell. The wild boars had returned to the womb of their mother. The roe deer had vanished into the medieval stave of blind paths. The sky, curly, with heavy bags under its eyes, wrestled with tormented melancholy.

In such desolation, the horse's breath was a hearth.

The escort of the 300 crows of Xallas waited at the entrance to the village, and the knight saw the large sow nuzzling in the mud, chewing the rainbow of the dirty waters. It let him go past, indifferent, not even raising its false little eyes. There were no figures leaning against the double doors nor silhouettes hidden behind the curtains. The world had forgotten the art of looking outside. Through a window, Simón saw the grandfather of grandfathers separating kernels in front of the television. In another house, a whole family was glued to the screen, munching at a table in silence. They passed down the main street and were ignored, as if they had arrived late for the beginning of summer time.

Albar came to a halt in front of Beatriz's house. Since no-one appeared, Simón went and rapped on the horseshoe knocker. From inside the house came the deafening uproar of gunfire, car tyres screeching around a bend, police sirens, energetic voices anticipating a further round of shots. Evidently, all this was part of the silence. He heard the sound of someone dragging their feet and, in the spotlight projected by the day along the corridor, slowly there came into view the bony, stooped, mournful figure of someone who resembled Aunt María.

She was muttering under her breath, "It's him, of course it is, he's here." But giving Simón a wary look, she asked, "Who is it?" And then, "What do you want?"

Simón smiled bitterly. He wished with all his heart that this were a new game, a challenge, and that soon plump Aunt María would come bustling down the corridor, inviting him in, her voice ringing out for Bea to come downstairs, you've a visitor, hold him tight by the reins, don't let the horse get away, I don't suppose you'd like someone a bit more mature?

"Bea's not here," she said finally.

She gestured as if to close the door, but was impeded by Simón's iron arm. The visitor's eyes were red, illuminated with hearts and swords. She thought it would be wise to lower his blood pressure.

"Bea does not live with us any more, child. She's gone into service in Coruña."

It was clear that Simón was linking up the words. The uncle with the Havana hat appeared at the end of the corridor.

"Tell him the truth!"

"I already have! She's working as a maid. In Coruña. We don't know where she's staying. We don't want to know."

This time, she managed to close the upper leaf of the door without obstruction.

The knight spat out a miniature of snakes and shaken sentiments, mounted Albar, and they trotted off towards the north, combed by the wind, accompanied by the loyal escort of the 300 crows of Xallas, slovenly echoes of an avenging thunderclap.

42

Every day that went by, the fox got better, as was apparent from the way its wounds looked less nasty, its coat recovered its sheen, from its insatiable appetite and, above all, from the brightness of its eyes. Overcoming her initial disgust, it was Rosa who noticed the change most. These two flames burning inside the shed began to exert a strange influence on her, so that every hour she would ritually half-open the door and stand on the threshold, exchanging captive looks.

Since the discovery, Spiderman's presence in the house had become habitual. In addition to looking after the animal, with a careful routine of cures, meals and sun-baths, he continued with his plan for the adornment of the threshing floor. In the end, Rosa accepted his offer to paint the front of the house. Cholo, she said, had shrugged his shoulders at the idea and laughed scornfully, what with all that ludicrous business of children, fox and unemployed emigrant acting as veterinary surgeon. With her consent, Spiderman chose the colours of the houses in the local fishing villages, which were white for the walls and blue for the frames. At the top of the ladder, with his brush and zinc bucket, he would hum and whistle songs all day, in the way that painters do. *I don't know what it is about your eyes, I don't know what it is about your mouth, they turn my every wish into a cry and cause my heart to fall upon the grooooound.*

And that day Spiderman said that he would be eating out, even though Rosa was adamant that he stay. When he returned, passing the children on their way to school, he had on the borsalino, the wide brimmed felt hat he sometimes wore, and carried his jacket over one shoulder, holding it in the crook of his finger.

Standing at the gate of the threshing floor, he had seen the woman from behind, leaning against the door-frame of the shed, so involved with the animal that she did not even hear him approach until she felt his breath very close, on the nape of her neck, and the light surprised her, as he leant against the door-frame as well, holding out his sturdy arm at right angles. "Oh, is that you?" she asked, only glancing around, at the height of his bare chest, spattered with specks of whitewash. She did not want to turn right around because, with him behind her and looking into the animal's eyes, she felt a sensation of agreeable unrest. Had she turned around, no doubt he would have moved away and they would each have carried on with what they were doing. But she did not turn, quite the opposite, accidentally on purpose she swooned just enough, the slightest movement which brought body into contact with body. At that signal, the male pressed gently against her buttocks, and she pressed back. Rosa went inside the shed, into the animal's gaze, without turning, and he followed, flinging his jacket and hat to the ground and seizing her by the elbow so that they were facing one another and could embrace passionately, not knowing quite what to do, whether to scratch or bite, it had taken so long to reach a state of war, as she murmured, "What do you think you're doing," and he gasped, "Oh, God!"

43

"Albar took Simón along the old coastal path, avoiding cars and houses with people, along cart-tracks and paths soaked to the bone in the soft bed of the wood and ways interlinked by tiny singers hidden in the undergrowth. This line, easily visible for the 300 crows, guided them to the dolmen of Dombate and from there to the ancient fortress of Borneiro. From here, they dropped down to the fields of Neaño and found the River Anllóns becoming sea, in that way, my lord, that captivates the soul. In the wilderness of the ocean, we can see how the serene flow is possessed by an exalted heart."

"They should set up a beauty school on Mount Branco," said the king of Galicia melancholically.

"And then, my lord, having passed the reed-beds of Anllóns at Ponteceso, they continued towards the area of Corme, as far as the Serpent's Stone."

"Winged serpent!" exclaimed His Majesty. "How I wish I knew how to read that book of stone!"

"They carried on through Mens. You should have seen the knight galloping across that Roman land, the 300 warriors blazing up on high. In the fertile plain, the women waved their broad-brimmed straw hats, tied with black ribbon. They even went up as far as Santo Adrián to look out over Malpica."

"The three Sisargas!" added His Majesty. "The native land of the sea birds. Guillemots, gulls, cormorants!"

"And they stopped at Buño, the red landscape of clay, the ovens of the tile-kilns, the potters' quarter."

"The nobility of hands in this country!"

"The procession came to the Stone of the Ark, with its Breton corridor, and from there, against the north-easterly, they passed by the sandbanks of Bergantiños. Razo, Barrañán, Baldaio, my lord!"

"I know, Toimil, I know."

"Albar trotted along the edge of the sea, in the wake of plovers and whimbrels. This is where birds rest that come from the twilight of the world and are off to warm their blood on African coasts. Year after year."

"They must sing in Gaelic!"

"And in Finnish, my lord, and in Flemish and in Latvian."

"It's a pity not to know languages! Those stories of the north have a lot of flavour."

"Further on, from the top of the rocks, they saw Caión, that wild cradle from where our men once went hunting for whales. It would be a sad district today, my lord, were it not for the tragic countenance of the sea that makes it more beautiful. When they reached Arteixo, they suddenly found themselves in traffic. The cars whizzed past. The knight, with a portly bearing and hardened features, was wearing his walkman. He may have been listening to that song he liked so much:

> *Over the distant mountain*
> *a horseman rides out west,*
> *he's lonely in the world*
> *and longs for his own death."*

In Sabón by now, Albar approached the balcony of the last reed-bed, it's a wonder to watch mallards, teals and shearwaters still diving against the light by the factory buildings. In Pastoriza, they visited the shrine of Our Lady of farmers and fishermen. Then, in Bens, they could breathe a new desolation. The 300 crows cawed suddenly. The cauldrons of dusk appeared before their eyes. The gigantic industrial chimneys of the Oil Refinery seared the first veils of night. The sunset entered into combustion in the hood of the city. The cars that went by now were like impassive lancers that hurt their eyes. Soon, the escort's cawing began to merge with a tide of sounds spat out haphazardly in the luminous chaos. Only the rhythmic persistence of the trotting made itself heard over the din of horns, alarms and sirens, in such a way that there was a moment, on Finisterre Avenue, populous gate to the city, when all the noises went quiet to listen to Albar, and the 300 took up the call like souls in the neon sky. The traffic stopped at the roundabout to give the knight some room. In Pontevedra Square, rumour had it that a man was arriving on horseback, followed by a vast flock of crows.

In one corner of the Borrazas bar, his head certainly full of birds of omen, the poet Andy Brigo was composing a sonnet on the end of the world. For years he had been a member of the Graffiti gang, which had filled the city with such scribblings as: Long Live the Exact Sciences! or Scientists Have Not Replaced the Brave, signed by ORA (the Organization of Rationalist Art). The group had disbanded on account of a judicial order that condemned them to washing down the walls and buses of the city. During the trial, they had done their best to avoid being sentenced by declaring themselves to be artists. The judge preferred to describe their work as "an act of vandalism". In a later appeal, following their lawyer's advice, they declared themselves to be mad. The judge was delighted to accept this argument, defended with enthusiasm by a psychological expert who wrote his report after a conversation lasting two minutes. They were, therefore, acquitted as madmen and not as artists. The whole incident had left its indelible mark on Andy Brigo. Rehabilitated as a copywriter in an advertising agency, he came up daily with captions that were having great success due to their impact. He used his old graffiti as a source of inspiration, and now it graced hoardings in a beautiful and legal way. For example, THE LIMIT IS 60, DRIVE AT 100 (advertising campaign for the new young person's car), CAN YOU SWALLOW THIS? (special offers in a supermarket), BREAK WITH THE FILTHY SYSTEM (new brand of washing powder) or A MAN IS A NATION (campaign to raise institutional awareness for the collection of new taxes). Things were going well, but he felt a deep sense of uneasiness. Perhaps that is why he so enjoyed devoting the twilight hours in the Borrazas to writing his work *The Last Day Is Close*, a detailed description of the Apocalypse, which in Coruña would no doubt take the form of a collective drowning, with starfish sucking out the eyes of corpses, octopuses embracing modernist caryatids and crabs occupying shop windows stocked with sheer lingerie.

But before that, Brigo wrote, *King Arthur would arrive with an army of avenging carrion birds, themselves Knights of the Round Table.*

No sooner had he put this down on paper than he heard the announcement made by a man in a black leather jacket with silver studs, green and red hair and a pirate's ring in his ear, who from the door warned of the presence of a gaudy knight surrounded by an unusual flock of crows. Andy Brigo was stunned. Then, together with the rest of the gang, he went out in search of the herald, who had already attracted a train of admirers.

The 300 alighted on the roofs of the buildings which in Orzán look out to sea and at this point Simón dismounted and began ringing at the entryphones.

"Who is it?"

" . . ."

"Who's calling?"

" . . ."

"Hello, hello. Yes, who is it?"

" . . ."

Holding on to Albar by the reins, he pressed the buttons with his other hand and applied his ear in the hope of hearing his loved one's voice. His heart had taken him to that part of the city.

"Can I help you?"

" . . ."

"Who's doing this?"

" . . ."

"Is that you?"

" . . ."

At a safe distance and in silence, the witnesses followed Simón from one doorway to the next. The anonymous voices of the speakers began to get mixed up. They grew annoyed, repeated themselves, suddenly recognized one another.

"Who is it, who is it?"

"It's me. Who are you?"

"What do you mean, who am I? Who are *you*?"

"But, why are you asking who I am?"

"No one round here's asking."

"This is 9 A."

"You're 9 A? Why, I'm 4 C."

"Do you want to come up?"

"Come up? Where?"

"Vandals."

"That's right, vandals."

"What was that? Who's calling?"

Heads appeared at windows and berated the youngsters, to which they replied.

"Drunks!"

"Curs, scoundrels!"

"Up yours!"

"Who is it? Who is it?" repeated a solitary voice over the loudspeaker.

From a top floor, someone hurled a plastic bag full of water which cracked like a whip on the ground. From the street, they responded with empty cans that rang out against the windows. Unmoved by the fuss, Simón continued his journey along the line of entryphones. He did not even pay attention to the police siren. Suddenly, he felt a strong hand gripping his shoulder. He turned around. He was met by a puzzled gaze, fixed on his gaudy hat. He pushed him aside with his iron arm in such a way that the man in uniform tripped and fell. When they ordered him to halt, Simón had already mounted Albar, who galloped off towards the beach.

A crowd of curious onlookers approached the balustrade of the sea front in Orzán. At a run, stimulated by the neighbourly brawl, the members of the gang arrived. The police reinforcements finally opened a way through with short, sharp blasts on the siren. From one car, they produced a spotlight that searched for the white of the horse. Albar trotted lightly along the beach. Then he stopped and cut capers on the lace fringe of the waves. All attention was suddenly drawn towards the cloud of crows that descended, cawing, and flapped about the street lamps.

When they tried to locate the knight again, they could make out nothing.

"He disappeared out to sea!" said Brigo.

The policemen looked at him incredulously. His voice was hoarse and reeked of liquor. The lapel of his jacket, covered in badges. They knew who he was. A member of the Graffiti gang. Out to sea? Right!

"It was King Arthur, boys. You let him get away."

44

"That evening," Toimil informed the king of Galicia, "much earlier than usual, when night had yet to absorb Spiderman's colours from the walls, the master of the house returned, with the radio blaring inside the car. He had his own way of wearing a suit, the tie loosened around his neck, and he walked with a tinkle of coins and keys, with an air of determination that comes from not being completely drunk.

"The door was open. He already had his head inside the house when he stepped back and gave the front of the house a glance.

"Spiderman was holding the little boy and playing at bouncing him up and down on his knees. Next to him, at the table, the two elder children were doing their homework. In the kitchen, Rosa walked about in the warm calm of the steam from a stew. When Cholo finally entered, they all seemed to agree to smile, which far from pleasing the new arrival distanced him even further from the scene of a strange, happy family. Instinctively, he went and stood by the hearth."

"So, how's the animal getting on?" he asked.

"Fine, it's doing fine."

"Spiderman says it . . ."

"I like the new look you've given the house," he said, suddenly changing the subject. "You'll let me know how much I owe you."

"Oh, come off it. You don't owe me anything."

"What do you mean, I don't owe you anything? A job has to be paid for."

"No, Cholo. The agreement was for nothing."

"What agreement? You did a job, I'll pay you for it."

"No, honestly. It was just something I did, it wasn't a job or anything."

"A job's a job," he said with drunken wisdom.

Spiderman could feel his presence closer to him, his untrusting eyes piercing him. It was clear that he was not going to let him get away with this.

"A job always has to be paid for. It gets paid for, we have a drink, and everyone's happy."

"No, please, let's just leave it."

"How much do I owe you?" he insisted. He already had his wallet in his hand.

"Come on, Cholo, you don't owe me anything! It was simply a way of passing time."

"How much? Twenty, fifty . . . a hundred?"

Spiderman stood up and placed the child on the ground. Cholo held his hand out against the other's chest. In the depths of those eyes, Spiderman could see the boy who wanted to fish for trout by smacking the surface of the water with a stick.

"We're friends, Cholo."

"Not if you don't get paid."

"All right then."

He looked over at Rosa. In the corner. With her back to them, oblivious, in the steam. A pot with letters: Salt.

"All right then."

"That's more like it. How much?"

"I don't know. Whatever you want."

"30,000 pesetas? How does that sound? I think 30,000 should do it."

"30,000? OK. 30,000 it is."

"Now, we'll have a drink."

"Yeah, we'll have a drink."

"Of course we will! We'll drink to the health of our friend! Our friend from New York!"

And when Rosa approached silently, her eyes steamed up behind the tray, he asked, "By the way, when are you going back there?"

"Soon," said Spiderman.

The world was in the fishbowl of the glass, deformed by the wide angle. He could see her figure in the background. Ashamed, silent like an Indian woman in films. He took a long swig.

"Yeah, very soon. I got the contract today."

Then he finished the drink in another gulp and said that it was late, that night was closing in and he did not want to be a nuisance, to which the master of the house protested ritually and made as if to refill his glass. But Spiderman was already moving away and he said goodbye to everyone without looking at anyone in particular. And Rosa's goodbye was also such that she did not avert her eyes from the things she held in her hands in the sink, absorbed in the water's ballad.

"That night," Toimil recounted to the king of Galicia, "the light in the kitchen was a long time going out."

Rosa delayed going to bed for as long as she could. When the children were asleep, and even after her husband had cast off from the bottle and retired, she ironed what was in the basket and then she even sewed buttons and rips in the children's clothes. When she went up, she walked slowly, exorcizing the sleepy laments of the floorboards upstairs. She undressed beside the curtain, in the moonlight, and located the place on the bed furthest removed from the other who was snoring.

She had not closed her eyes, dreaming while still awake that she had reached sleep, an old bearded tramp who embraced her sweetly, when she noticed that her husband was turning over and had begun to fondle her. His hand moved carelessly and shamelessly, getting bigger, wider, more brutal. And it was followed by the rest of his body, let loose, panting through his mouth. She watched as sleep fled in horror, limping across the fields.

He felt her tense, ready to resist, protecting her sex with her thighs squeezed tight, her arms guarding her breasts, buttocks clenched. Desire grew in him with rage, a mechanical force, the pleasure of subduing, controlling, softening, opening, and making the soul in that enemy body cry out. When he saw that she would not yield despite his efforts and that she had two tears brimming in her eyes, he fell into a fury and gave her two slaps across the face with his open hand which sounded like cracks in the night, and then he mounted her, pushed as far as he could go, to where he had never reached before with his sword, levering himself with his elbows on solid ground, baring his teeth to those tearful, wide-open eyes.

When he collapsed and turned into a dead weight, all the force that had been roused during the combat thronged inside her chest. Wandering desperately through the fields after the sweet lord of sleep, she found a trail of bloodied flowers, petals that were tears of eyes stuck in the ground, twitching fruit unearthed by the wound of an iron plough. She moved away from the man with disgust. She felt the sticky patch of his sweat with shame. She was wide awake and hurting. The moonlight, through the curtain, embroidered the room with shadow play. She got up, opened the wardrobe and took the pistol from the chest of jewels. She returned to the bed and ran the barrel over the man's silhouette. She was not thinking and she was not afraid. The shadows swelled slightly over the photograph of her mother and brought it to life.

"Girl," said her mother, "what time is it?"

"Late, Mum. Go to sleep."

"What about you?"

"I can't sleep."

"Don't do it, girl. You'll stain everything. You won't get the sheets clean. Blood is very difficult to wash out."

"Sleep, Mum."

"The sky was so lit up by the moon," Toimil told the king of Galicia, "that birds were fooled into chirping in the bay trees. She went outside, wearing her husband's jacket over her nightdress. It was cold. In the light of the new moon, everything becomes expectant. She crossed the threshing floor in the direction of the shed. When she opened the door, a luminous blast of the night's lamp entered with her and the animal turned with twinkling eyes."

"So you're not asleep either. Are you?"

She knew those eyes. She knew their secret. Tender and proud, sweet and wild. She bent down and placed her hand on its head, unafraid. The fox allowed her to stroke the nape of its neck and the white patch of fur under its mouth, which was closed with docile bitterness.

Then Rosa stood up and pointed to the door, freedom, the moon. "Go! Go on, go!" The animal did not even move. Rosa tried to lift it up, first pushing it, then taking hold of its ribs, but the fox moaned and collapsed in a heap. Rosa wept. She stroked it and wept.

"I won't let you suffer this time. No, madam, I won't let you suffer."

"And it's true that not a sound was heard, not even a whimper," said Toimil to the king of Galicia, "only the click of the weapon. It was what is known as a clean shot."

45

The bell realized that an inexpert hand had hold of the clapper. It was making it ring in a mad, irregular, playful fashion. It had been quiet for many years now except when there was a funeral, but there had been a time when, as well as death, it had announced with varied music all the important events in Arán: Masses, births, the village festival, the fire, harvests, dawn, the angelus. The old men working the fields uncovered their heads reverentially and looked in the direction of the belfry, surprised, however, by the precipitate peals. They were just some kids who wanted to say goodbye with cheer.

"Get down from there!" Rosa called from the porch.

"We're leaving, we're leaving for the city!" they shouted in the direction of the fields.

She should also have been happy, but she entered the church with a sense of unease. The altars were empty, the absence of the images marked by the dusty silhouettes on the walls. The virgins of Arán – Saint Mary, Our Lady of Sorrows, the Assumption, the Immaculate Conception, Our Lady of Succour, the Annunciation, Our Lady of Hope – were kept in the houses of villagers for fear of the raiders of temples who had already plundered chapels and parish churches in the vicinity. No Masses were said. The more devout parishioners attended Sunday services in Néboa. The priest, who had the care of seven parishes and worked in a bank, only came to Arán to administer the last blessing to the deceased. From time to time, strangers arrived, especially in the summer, to see the paintings, the beautiful ladies shown in the fresco of Arán. But these saintly sinners suffered from the elements more than anyone. The green swathes of damp were covering up the colours and concealing the figures, including the skeleton and archer of death. Only Rosa could see them, reconstruct them with her eyes. She turned to the high altar, aware of a presence. There was a mouse next to the altar-table. It remained still. It seemed to be looking at her, but she did not flinch. Nor did she do anything to frighten it.

Before I go, she thought, I should sweep the floor and put out some flowers.

"She stood watching me, my lord," said Toimil to the king of Galicia. "Not fleetingly, as she had done before. She was on her way back from the ruins of the manor, holding a bunch of camellias in her hand. She stopped and raised her eyes towards me. I've never seen her looking so beautiful. I don't know if I shall be able to live without her!"

A jet-black crow flew in from the scarecrow where it had been on guard and alighted beside them, on the chimney.

"They're going, Simón," said the king of Galicia. "Now, we're the only ones left."

"There's a storm on the way, my lord!" announced the watch of the 300.

"Attention!" cawed His Majesty. And immediately he gave the order with daring resolve, "Against the wind!"